# KAFKA IN A SKIRT

Camino del Sol

*A Latina and Latino Literary Series*

DANIEL CHACÓN

# Kafka in a Skirt

## STORIES FROM THE WALL®

**THE UNIVERSITY OF
ARIZONA PRESS**

TUCSON

The University of Arizona Press
www.uapress.arizona.edu

© 2019 by Daniel Chacón
All rights reserved. Published 2019

ISBN-13: 978-0-8165-3991-8 (paper)

Cover design by Leigh McDonald

Publication of this book is made possible in part by the proceeds of a permanent endowment created with the assistance of a Challenge Grant from the National Endowment for the Humanities, a federal agency.

Library of Congress Cataloging-in-Publication Data
Names: Chacon, Daniel, author.
Title: Kafka in a skirt : stories from the wall / Daniel Chacon.
Other titles: Camino del sol.
Description: Tucson : The University of Arizona Press, 2019. | Series: Camino del Sol, a Latina and Latino literary series
Identifiers: LCCN 2018054038 | ISBN 9780816539918 (pbk. : alk. paper)
Subjects: LCSH: Mexican Americans—Fiction. | LCGFT: Short stories.
Classification: LCC PS3553.H215 A6 2019 | DDC 813/.54—dc23 LC record available at https://lccn.loc.gov/2018054038

Printed in the United States of America
♾ This paper meets the requirements of ANSI/NISO Z39.48-1992 (Permanence of Paper).

For Lucinda Jolène Chacón

*I hope that when you're old enough to read this book, you won't think your daddy too crazy. As of this writing, I haven't seen you, but as you tumble around inside my soulmate's belly, I sing to you and read you stories. That's my voice you hear.*

*It says,* I love you.

*Aun si digo sol y luna y estrella me refiero a cosas que me suceden.*

—ALEJANDRA PIZARNIK

*¡Señor Alcalde, sus hijas están mirando a la luna!*

—LORCA

# THE ORDER OF THINGS

## Part Three

## Part Four

# KAFKA IN A SKIRT

# PART ONE

# IN THE CLOSET

Mom barged into my room and started sweeping and commanding me to pick up this T-shirt, that shoe.

"And *that*!" she yelled, pointing inside my closet.

"What?"

"¡Esta chingadera!"

"Chinga-what? ¿Qué es . . . ?"

"Throw it away, you pig!"

I looked inside the closet, and I was afraid of what I might see, but I didn't see anything that looked like it might be called a chingadera.

She hit me on my leg with the broom. "¡Cochino!" It stung.

"¡Tíralo!"

I got on my knees to find the chingadera.

I didn't know what I was looking for, but I somehow knew I would spend the rest of my life hiding it.

# THE *HIDDEN* ORDER OF THINGS

I recall a story about Sandra Cisneros's reaction when critics of her novel *Caramelo* claimed she was being "experimental" by using footnotes and other "postmodern" literary devices.

She responded, That's not experimental. That's Mexican!

I'm not sure if this story is true, but I want it to be, and it makes sense.

I'm going to provide suggestions on the paths one can take walking through the rooms of this collection, a technique that echoes both Ana Castillo and Julio Cortázar, two great Latinx writers who have done this in *The Mixquiahuala Letters* and *Rayuela,* respectively. These alternative paths are therefore not "experimental" or an attempt to be "postmodern"; rather, they are a Latinx perspective on multiple ways of experiencing a text.

## Path One:

If you look for thematic meanings in a text, this would be the way to read it:

> Kafka in a Skirt
> The Truth About the Wall*

The Furry Spider
Water and Dog
Every Book Is a Wormhole
Running Through a Museum
The Enchanted Tiki Room
A Death of Time

After reading the above stories in that order, please refer back to the original Order of Things as a way in which to finish the rest of the book.

## Path Two:

If you spent your childhood imagining that you could enter into other dimensions, if you imagined walking into a mirror and finding a reverse universe, or you wanted to find a secret passage in your house, like a panel in the floor of some dark closet at the end of the hallway, then the following order would work best:

Kafka in a Skirt
The Cauldron
The Enchanted Tiki Room
A Young City
Every Book Is a Wormhole
The *And Ne Forhtedon Ná!*
A Nice Baguette
A Stupid Cow
Water and Dog
You Can't Do That with a Goat!
The Third Reason
The Barbarians
Running Through a Museum
A Death of Time

After reading the above stories in that order, you can refer back to the original Order of Things.

## Path Three:

This is a work of Chicano literature. Most readers will know that before they buy the book or before they open it, and Chicano literature is one of the fibers of the Latinx literary fabric. If you are interested in what makes this book "Chicano," why it is *Latinx* literature as opposed to just *literature* or *American literature,* this would be the best way to enter the book:

> Kafka in a Skirt
> Bien Chicano
> Fuck Shakespeare
> I Did Like Ricky
> Lady of the Silver Lake
> It's the Eschatology!
> Six Cows in a Spaceship

After reading the above stories in that order, do whatever you want with the rest of them.

## Path Four:

Open the table of contents and skim over the titles. If one strikes you, say "The Cauldron" or "Furry Spider," read it.

This is the best way to read this book.

# BIEN CHICANO

I'm going to bring eggrolls, Tran said. Vietnamese style. The white people will go crazy. They love eggrolls!

I bet they're delicious, said Soul, but I'm going to bring a Hmong soup that I'm sure none of you guys have ever tasted.

Lucy said, with a big smile and a bit embarrassed, I'm a white girl! I'm going to bring macaroni and cheese!

It was Lucy, the community college's affirmative action director, whose idea it was to have a potluck, and she told everybody they needed to bring a dish that would represent their culture.

We were all poor, at-risk students, and it was her job to help us graduate or transfer to a four-year university.

Becca said she would bring baba ghanoush, and Chuck promised fry bread, traditional style from the rez.

Lucy wrote down what everyone would bring, an ethnic salpicón, a taste of America. She was excited.

She turned to me and said, What will you bring, Eddy? Tacos? Nachos?

Immediately one of my childhood favorites came to mind, like Tía Lupita used to make for us when we visited her unexpectedly, but I wasn't sure if it was the right choice, so I told Lucy I would bring something ¡bien Chicano! Something I grew up with.

On the list under "Eddy," Lucy wrote, *Something Bien Chicano*.

I arrived to the potluck with a tray of bologna sandwiches on white bread with lots of mayonnaise, and when I say white bread, I mean working-class Bimbo Bread, those loaves that are so soft when you first open them, and they have so many preservatives they last more than two months.

And the bologna was Bar-S, the cheap brand.

That's not Mexican! Tran said, laughing at my bologna sandwiches.

Just like Tía Lupita used to make, I said. She was *not* a traditional Mexican woman.

But it was *supposed* to be about tradition, said Lucy, disappointed. It was supposed to represent your cultural heritage.

But bologna is my culture!

Bologna! said Lucy. You said you would bring something *bien Chicano*. She was trying to pretend like she was kidding, trying to keep it light, but I could tell she really was perturbed with me, as if I didn't take cultural diversity seriously enough. I wanted to go up to her and say I was sorry, because I liked Lucy and I know she wanted to help us. Whenever we had an issue with a racist professor or trouble communicating with the administration, she was there for us, fighting for us. But I was also a little irritated at her, so I decided to just ignore her feelings.

When it was time to eat, everyone uncovered their dishes to the oohs! and ahhs! of the others, like what they had brought was something to be proud of, and the smells were great. Tran looked over my plate of bologna sandwiches on white bread and said, I can't believe you brought this! And she grabbed one, ate it, and as she chewed, she looked like she was about to say something. Not bad, she said, and she had another one. Then Soul ate one or two or three, and then Becca ate a few, and everyone, as they ate them, would say things like, So let's see about this Chicano food, like they were making fun of me, but they kept eating the bologna sandwiches, everyone except for Lucy.

When Tran told her she should try one, that they were actually pretty good, Lucy said, No thanks! She was serving herself more eggrolls. She looked at my sandwiches and shook her head, disappointed.

After we were all done eating, there was still a lot of food left over, fry bread, pozole, hummus, even eggrolls, but there were no more bologna sandwiches.

# FURRY SPIDER

When I opened my eyes, I saw Bacon on my chest playing with some-thing, like a string. As my eyes focused, I could see that it was a spider, legs twinkling in the moonlight, trying to run up my chest. Bacon kept pushing it back with his claws and playing with it.

I hate spiders, so I screamed and jumped out of bed.

That woke up my wife, and she was angry because she has to get up at five a.m. every morning and drive an hour to work.

"What the hell's going on?" she snapped.

"Bacon brought a spider to bed!"

"You're dreaming," she said. "Again."

Not even thirty seconds later, she started to snore, but I couldn't crawl back into that bed knowing that somewhere in the sheets or blankets there was a spider waiting to bite into me like I was a slab of tuna.

The next night it happened again, Bacon brought a big spider to my bed. I don't know what kind it was, maybe a brown recluse, but I saw the silhouette of it running across my chest, and I screamed and jumped out of bed, and my wife woke up again.

"You idiot!" she yelled. "Let me sleep!" She turned her back to me, and her snoring started seconds later.

I went into the living room and sat in an armchair, looking around the floors and walls for deadly spiders. I got up and opened a bottle of wine, poured a glass, and stood looking out the sliding glass doors at the city lights. And suddenly I understood.

We lived in a house in the desert mountains, and we had a view of El Paso and Ciudad Juárez, miles and miles of flat city lights and beyond to the mountains. Our house was ultramodern, a "smart home," but it was so high in the desert that we would inevitably get a lot of spiders, even tarantulas that would crawl from the terrain onto our lawn. I don't care how many people tell me they're not dangerous, they creep me out, and I kill them with a shovel and then go into the house and lock the sliding glass doors. I won't go out in the backyard for weeks, even though there's a pool back there.

In the desert mountains there are also scorpions, a lot of them, and we hear stories from neighbors about finding them in dark corners of their garages or in their boots.

Bacon meowed and rubbed against my ankles so I would open the glass doors, but I wouldn't do it, because he would run out there and grab some spiders to bring home. I poured another glass of wine and sat in an armchair. I couldn't help but imagine that if I fell asleep Bacon would bring me a scorpion to play with. It would crawl up my face and bite me in the eye. I also feared the brown recluse, a deadly spider native to the region. How ironic that I finally made enough money to live in a dream house with a beautiful view, but it had more deadly spiders than my childhood home in Fresno, where I grew up squashing cockroaches and chasing rats with baseball bats.

Bacon jumped on my lap and it startled me, and I spilled my wine. "Fucking Bacon!" I said, standing up, the red liquid dripping from my chest like a wound. I poured another glass.

When I met my wife, she was an underpaid professor of child development, but after tenure and three years as department chair, she became a dean and started making lots of money.

I worked at home for The Wall', a data storage company, but she had to drive across the city and arrive at work early in the morning and stay there all day. One time, less than a year before the beginning of this story, she called me around ten a.m., which was unusual because she was always too busy to call during the day. Before I answered, I turned down the volume of the music. I was listening to classic punk.

"Are you home?" she asked.

"Where else?" I said. "I'm an anarchist."

"I have something I need to show you."

"What is it?" I asked.

"I'll be home for lunch," she said.

It was, of course, a little black Bombay kitten, adorable but with a slight asshole smirk on his face, as if right from the beginning he was telling us, "I'm gunna fuck with you."

I made my amazing BLTs for lunch, which I know my wife loves, and after throwing around ideas for names, Bumble Bee, Bigger, Quark, I pulled a strip of bacon from my sandwich and threw it on the floor for the kitten. We watched him tear into it with his fangs like a lion into the belly of an antelope, and we both said at the same time, *Bacon!*

The first few days, she regretted bringing him home, because he was the kind of evil cat that comic strips are written about. He was mischievous as fuck, keeping us up at night playing with cups that he rolled across the tile, or he pulled boxes from shelves and watched them crash all over the floors. One time, we found him standing on the top of a bookcase where he knew he wasn't supposed to be, and he looked right at us, from her to me. Then he casually—and with clear intent—knocked a wineglass off. It hit the floor, and the glass shattered and the wine splattered. He kept looking right at us, as if to ask, "What you gunna do about it?"

We might have gotten rid of him if it wasn't for those rare moments when he would jump on our lap, curl up on our chest as close to our face as possible, and purr and let us scratch his neck. During those moments my wife quit thinking about how much she hated him, and she wouldn't budge while he was on her.

"Look!" she'd say, all excited as Bacon curled up under her chin. "He's letting me pet him!"

One night at dinner I told her that he had to go, that he was bringing spiders to bed, and she knew how much I hated spiders. I couldn't get any sleep.

"Bacon can be an asshole," she said. "But he wouldn't do that."

"I'm not making this up," I said.

"I tell you what," she said. "We'll keep our door shut tonight."

So we kept the door closed, but Bacon meowed and cried until three in the morning when my wife got up and opened the door. "I fucking hate you," she said as Bacon ran in. "Bastard kitty!"

He jumped on my chest.

Bacon was so close to my face that I could hear him breathe. His breathing always sounded forced, like he had asthma, and he wasn't purring. The orbs in his eyes were shiny black, only a few inches away from my eyeballs.

As soon as my wife flopped back on the mattress, she fell asleep.

I gently pushed Bacon off and got up and poured a glass of wine and sat in the armchair, and he jumped on the arm and looked at me. I stayed up all night.

My lack of sleep started to get to me, and during the day I couldn't think very well. I was absent-minded, forgetting things, like which code I was working on. I could be deep inside that language for two or three hours every morning, but by noon my mind goes *pop!* And I can't think that way anymore. All I see on my screen are a bunch of numbers and symbols, like secret writing from a demonic society.

One morning, I walked out the front door to stand in the back-yard, accidently locking the bottom lock.

It was a "smart" home, so all I had to do was open the app on my iPhone and unlock the door, but I left my phone inside too.

I didn't remember my wife's phone number, which was in my phone under "Cuddle Bunny," so I couldn't call her from a neigh-bor's house. I could call the university, but her admin assistant always answered and it took her all day to call me back.

The walk down the hill and into the city would have taken hours, and it was summer and I was barefoot. My feet were so tender I could hardly walk across the grass, let alone trek across miles of burning concrete and cement like a holy man. I went into the backyard and jumped into the pool. It felt too cold. I shivered until I warmed up. The sun was intense on my head.

We had a half refrigerator back there, but all it had was beer, so by two p.m. I was drunk.

By three p.m. I was dehydrated and hot and miserable. I tried to open the sliding glass door to get back in, and Bacon stood on the other side watching me, not even concerned that I might die. He had a slight smirk on his face.

When my wife got home she found me on a lawn chair glowing red like a department store Santa.

"You look like shit," she said.

"Just let me the fuck in," I said.

When I got into the house I drank a gallon of cold water, and I knew I wanted to kill Bacon.

One night in bed in the dark my wife said, "Honey, you need help. This isn't healthy. Your fear of spiders is . . ."

"It's not fear," I said. "Bacon *is* bringing spiders to bed!"

"Then how come we never found a spider in the sheets?"

"I don't know," I said. "Imagine you're the size of a spider and there's this giant creature dragging you around in its teeth. Wouldn't you want to get away?"

"You're imagining all this."

"I know what I saw."

"Okay, look, you're not getting any sleep anyway. *You* stay awake. But in bed. Don't go into the other room and drink wine all night. Maybe we'll see that this alleged spider epidemic—"

"Real spider!" I said.

"Fine, with the fucking real spider you can wake me up. I won't get mad."

"You mean like you are now?" I asked.

"I promise. Just show me the spider."

"Okay," I said, and she nuzzled her face into my chest and told me she loved me. I kissed her forehead and she moved her head up and we kissed on the lips. She put her hand down there.

She wasn't subtle when she wanted sex. We made love. It was nice.

I fell asleep and woke up the next morning when my wife's alarm clock went off at five a.m.

"See?" she said. "You imagined the spiders!"

The next night it happened again. We made love, I fell asleep, and I woke up to her alarm clock.

But then one night Bacon came through the bedroom door, jumped on my chest, and I saw a huge spider dangling from his teeth. Before he could drop it on my chest, I yelled, "Look! Look!" and woke up my wife.

I shone the flashlight on Bacon's fangs.

Trapped in his teeth was a scrunchie, a furry rubber band that my wife used to hold back her hair. He put it on my chest and began to play with it.

"See?" my wife said. "There's no spider!"

"But, but . . ." I didn't know what to say.

"There's not so many spiders in this house that he can bring you one every night," she said, like trying to calm down a mental patient.

"They're everywhere," I said. "Did you know, you're never more than two inches away from a spider? Ever! And while you're sleeping, you swallow at least three hundred spiders a year."

"You told me that exact same thing last week."

"I did not!"

"Did too. You just drank too much wine to remember."

"That's ridiculous."

"No! Ridiculous is believing we swallow three hundred spiders a year."

"I don't remember the exact number, but it's high."

For the next few days I watched Bacon closely, staying up all night, sometimes going through two bottles of wine.

One night, he jumped on the armrest with another scrunchie. I flicked it across the room and he jumped off the bed and chased after it, grabbed it in its teeth, ran back, jumped up, and dropped it on my lap for another round. One time he brought it back I thought it was a spider—only for half a second, but long enough for me to jerk my body and spill the wine.

Then one day, after spending three hours inside the coding world, I was sitting out by the pool.

Bacon was walking around the backyard snapping his teeth at birds, and I jumped into the water. I crawled out and dripped my way to the little refrigerator, and I started on my first beer.

I listened to classic punk, danced around to a few songs, *I wanna be sedated!* Had more beer and then switched to a cold bottle of Chardonnay, which was gone before I knew it, and I had to go back to beer. At one point I must have turned off the music, but I don't remember much after singing *I want to be anarchy!* so loud the neighbors' dogs started barking, but I must have decided to lay on the chair next to the pool, under an umbrella, and obviously I fell asleep.

I had no idea how long I was out, but when I opened my eyes there were two tarantulas on the pool deck, on either side of me.

I was unable to move, but I screeched such a piercing sound the neighbors' dogs started barking, which made me panic even more.

My wife doesn't believe this part of the story, but I looked around and saw tarantulas and other spiders all over the lawn, crawling toward me with intention. I imagined them strapping me to the ground like I was Gulliver and excavating my body of meat and blood.

The fear in my chest felt like a large, metal ball. Then Bacon showed up.

I remember at first he started playing with the tarantulas, pushing them against each other, and they tried to get away, but he kept pushing them back. Then I remember he picked one up in his teeth and ran across the lawn, jumped the little fence that separates our yard from the desert mountains, dropped the tarantula, and came back and picked up the other one and did the same. Then he zigzagged across the lawn like quick, black strokes of a Motherwell and picked up spiders, and when all the spiders were gone, he walked around the yard and found a spot on the grass and rolled around in it.

The next day I was too hungover to get any work done, so after my wife left for the university I went back to bed.

Before I dozed off, Bacon came in, this time with one of my wife's bracelets dangling in his teeth. He jumped on my chest and dropped the bracelet and looked at me.

I scratched him on the head, and he let me. He collapsed his legs and lay on my chest, and he inched his way to my chin and purred and he let me scratch his neck, his eyes closed in pleasure. I scratched his neck, his butt, his spine. He wiggled under my touch like a furry spider, then he curled into my armpit and fell asleep.

# A NICE BAGUETTE

Cohen took a piece of bread, pushed it against the spaghetti, and twirled the noodles with his fork. He brought them to his mouth and was about to eat the first bite of the night when he heard, "Can I have a piece of bread?"

For years he sat at his kitchen table to eat dinner, the window pushed open and no screen between him and the sidewalk, where people waited for the buses. Sometimes there were mobs of people right outside his window, inches from where he sat alone at his table and ate, but no one ever bothered him. No one looked into his window for very long. Obviously people saw him, but he didn't care, because all he ever saw of them were bodies and blurred faces sliding by, ghosts pouring in and out of buses. No one bothered him.

Until today.

The man stood at his window, framed by it. He held his head down in humility, but he looked up at Cohen with big eyes.

"What did you say?" barked Cohen.

"A piece of bread? Please?"

Cohen sighed, sat back in his chair, and looked at the baguette he had on the table. He violently pulled off a chunk, stood up, and handed it to the beggar.

"Now get lost," he said.

The beggar, keeping his head bowed in humility, thanked Cohen with his eyes.

Cohen sat down, and he noticed the butter dish on the table next to the bread. He looked out and saw that the man was away from the window, standing on the sidewalk and eating the bread with two hands—small, quick bites, like a squirrel chewing on an acorn.

Cohen tore off another piece of the baguette, ripped it open like a carcass, and spread butter up and down the insides. He walked to the window, handed it to the man.

The man happily accepted and whispered, "Thanks to the Mother."

"That one's got butter," Cohen said matter-of-factly, and he sat down to finish his dinner.

Far across the room, directly in front of him at the end of the narrow living room, the TV was on, without sound. He preferred the noise outside, the airbrakes of buses, the sirens, the buzz of conversations, the general human tumult of the city.

There was some stupid talk show on TV. A young woman was sitting in an armchair in a tiny dress, two very old men interviewing her, one on each side of her. She was animated and bubbly, but the old men seemed more interested in what she was wearing than what she was saying.

Cohen took a bite of spaghetti, and as he chewed, he looked out at the beggar, who was still eating like a squirrel.

He looked at his bottle of Bonarda, half full. It was a cheap brand, three and a half pesos, but the bottle's value for him was how it kept time. One bottle lasted two days, and he measured the days of the week by the number empty bottles in the corner of the kitchen.

He looked at the man, who was done eating. "Hey! Hey, you!"

"Yes, sir?" asked the beggar, walking up to the window and looking in, framed like a living painting in Harry Potter.

"You want something to drink?"

He nodded his head humbly, his eyes looking up at Cohen, and he said, "Yes, please."

Cohen sighed. He got up and took a plastic cup from the shelf, poured half a glass of the red wine, and then he filled the other half with fizzy water and handed it over.

"It's better with soda," he said. "It's not a great wine."

The man held the cup with both hands like a chalice and closed his eyes as he drank. "It's very good," he said.

"You want more bread? I could put ham in it. Do you like ham?"

"I don't eat ham," the man said. "Perhaps you might have some sliced turkey?"

"I got tuna," Cohen said, feeling a bit irritated. The man should have been happy with the ham.

Cohen made him a tuna sandwich with mustard, and he put it on a paper towel and handed it out the window.

"Praise the Mother," said the beggar. Cohen watched him eat.

"My name's Cohen," he said.

The beggar nodded, but he didn't tell his own name, he just ate the sandwich with one hand and drank the Bonarda with the other. The beggar looked content, like nothing could be better, and Cohen decided he shouldn't be irritated by him.

"You live around here?"

"I live in the provinces. I'm waiting for the bus, but with traffic it's over two hours to get back, and I saw you, and I'm sorry, but I saw the beautiful bread you had on your table and I thought of how hungry I was."

"55? 69? 127?"

"55."

"Well, they come pretty often. You can keep the cup."

The beggar nodded. Cohen grunted.

He went back to his chair, sat before the bowl of spaghetti, saw the second half of the baguette, and thought, "Yeah. It's a really nice baguette."

On TV, the young woman in the tiny dress was dancing, but the old men stayed seated in the leather armchairs, clapping and enjoying the show. From the sidewalk, people couldn't see the TV, but they could see Cohen, and he often imagined himself framed in the window like a painting, a bald, heavy man with large wrists and small hands eating at the table. Above him there hung a cheap painting on the wall, one he had bought at a flea market. It was a horse eating grass, a cheap copy, he knew, but he liked it.

He looked at the horse eating. He looked outside. "I have dulce de leche," he said.

The beggar didn't seem to notice because he was facing another direction, savoring the wine. He had a good profile, a strong nose, high cheekbones. He was good-looking. The five-o'clock shadow made him kind of ruggedly handsome. And he looked familiar, not like Cohen had met him before or had seen him a few times in the street, but as if his face, the way he looked into the sky as if content with the clouds, the entire aura that surrounded him, suggested that he was someone Cohen should know.

"I said I have dulce de leche," Cohen said.

"Really?" the man said, as if he couldn't believe what he was hearing.

"Do you like dulce de leche?"

"Very much, thank you. Praise the Mother."

The crowds outside the window grew larger, rush hour at its peak, and there were maybe fifty people out there, but they were all blurs of color and sound, except for the man. He was thin, but not skinny, with wide shoulders and a long neck.

"There's my bus," he said.

"They come every fifteen minutes," Cohen said, handing him bread spread thick with dulce de leche. "If you need to use the toilet or something . . ."

"I have to be going."

"You got kids?"

"Four," said the man. "From three to nine."

"And a wife?"

"Yes, of course. She's an angel."

"Do you got money for the bus?"

"Oh, yes," said the man. He put his hand into his pant pocket and pulled out some coins. "Like I said, there was something about that baguette. I don't usually do this."

"Okay, well, a have good day," Cohen said, and he sat back down to finish his meal, but the spaghetti was cold.

He looked straight ahead at the TV and was irritated by the old men watching the young woman dance, clapping their hands, looking at each other and winking, raping her with their eyes. He felt a surge of hatred for them. He wanted to change the channel, but he was tired, and the remote seemed so far. He looked away, out the window, and could see the buses lining up, people filing in, 127, 69, 55, and he saw the beggar sitting near the bus window, framed by it, eating the bread. He was right next to Cohen's window, parallel to him, like they were in different seats, going in the same direction.

# THE BARBARIANS

The rent was a little steep for their income, but Mike Gonzalez and Willow Martinez moved into a loft in the "hip" warehouse district south of downtown. Willow, a strict vegetarian, loved that she could walk to the farmer's market on Wednesdays and Saturdays, and there were bakeries and green restaurants all along the streets, and at night the jazz clubs spilled sax and piano into the neon tunnels leading to their loft.

Mike's commute to work was more difficult, since he had to pass through downtown and had to sometimes be inside his car in traffic for more than an hour, but Willow, a work-at-home artist, would be able to work well in the loft, a former leather factory. It had ceiling-high windows all around, so there was plenty of natural light, and on a clear day the mountains and hills surrounded the city like white elephants.

The first morning at the new loft, Mike woke up and went to touch Willow, since they made love almost exclusively in the mornings, but she wasn't in bed. He figured she was in her studio, working in the morning light.

He smelled something coming from the street, a scent that was good and familiar, almost comforting, as if the smell carried a memory he had lost, but before he could think about what it might be, he heard moaning from the bathroom. The door was open.

Willow, bent over the toilet, retched into it. "Can you believe that shit?" she said.

"You're pregnant?"

"No! That smell!"

"Oh, yeah." Still outside the bathroom door, he took in a big whiff, his nostrils flaring. "Nice. What is it?"

"Nice?? It's meat, Michael! Burning fucking flesh!"

The new restaurant across the street was a barbeque joint called The Barbarians, a city favorite that had opened up a new location. Their specialty was their "world famous" slow-cooked brisket, which they started making each day at three in the morning, so by seven a.m. the entire street smelled like sweet, salty meat.

Willow was so repulsed that she threw up that morning and the next, but Mike secretly liked it.

It had been her choice to be vegetarians, but before there was her, he had loved sinking his teeth into juicy meats. Sometimes, when he left town on business, he would visit an In-N-Out Burger like a man visits a brothel, guilty and excited and careful to hide the evidence. For the next few days, he brushed his teeth several times a day so she wouldn't smell it on him when he returned home.

When they were dating, she wouldn't kiss him after he ate meat, sometimes days after, pushing him away and saying she could taste dead animal on his tongue.

"It's so disgusting!"

"It was just one burger."

"You're like kissing roadkill."

Willow was a beautiful woman, not casually beautiful but stunningly beautiful, and Mike, who was plain and not very charismatic, would get a lot of looks when they were together in public. He'd had a belly, but once they married she made him work on it, supervising sit-ups and making him run with her in the evenings. He also used to smoke, which she made him quit, and he used to eat meat every meal, bacon or chorizo for breakfast, stacked New York deli–style sandwiches for lunch, and steaks and ribs for dinner, with several pints of heavy brown ale.

He was on the team that designed special effects for a movie studio, and he made enough so that Willow was able to work full time on her art. She occasionally sold a piece, but her goal was not to make money but to make statements, a lot of them. She even had a series she called *Meat Is Murder*, using quotes from the Morrissey anti-meat-eating song across images of brutality.

They complained to the landlord about the smell of the meat across the street, but he told them there was nothing he could do. They had paid the deposit and committed to a yearlong lease, and he had taken the loft off the market.

"Why didn't you tell us The Barbarians were coming?" Mike asked.

"I can't be here for a year," Willow said, holding her stomach, which Mike imagined she was holding gently because of pregnancy. He watched her hands splayed on her belly, her thin fingers.

"My hands are tied," the landlord said.

"We'll get a lawyer," she said.

While the lawyer negotiated with the company that owned the building, Willow stayed at her sister's house in Santa Monica and Mike stayed alone in the loft. Each morning, around seven-thirty, right when he woke up, the blood rushed to his erect penis and the brisket released its sweet scent. He couldn't help himself, he loved waking up to that.

Then one evening it happened.

That's how he would tell it: "It happened."

Not "He did it" or "He decided," but "It happened," as if he had no control over the plot of his own story.

*It just so happened* that one evening he walked out the door of their apartment and into the freight elevator, down to the bottom, out the front doors, and across the street to The Barbarians.

He sat at a table in the corner and ordered the brisket. Oh, how juicy it was, the best meat he had ever tasted.

He ate the whole thing with buttered bread, corn on the cob, and a pitcher of beer. His belly was so full he had to unbutton his pants.

He talked on the phone with Willow that evening, and she sounded maudlin and ironic, which meant she was working on a project, perhaps an abstract sculpture protesting Trump's border wall, but he didn't ask her about it, because all he wanted to do was take off his pants, lay in bed on his back, let his stomach grow like a magic mountain, and pass out.

"You sound different," she said.

"Just tired," he said.

The next day it happened again, and the next day it happened again, and it happened again and it happened again.

The lawyer got a settlement from the owners of the building. They would move Mike and Willow into another loft down the street in another building they owned, a former warehouse where the smell couldn't reach them.

This place was even more beautiful, with windows all around from ceiling to floor and overlooking the downtown skyline and beyond the vast East Side all the way to the mountains in the blurry distance. "I can work here," she said.

One night, the same day he had snuck a Smash Burger for lunch, Mike found Willow standing in front of the glass walls of the loft looking at the moon.

It was full and stunning, like a giant egg hanging over the city. It was so bright it shone on her face, and he saw an expression that he had only seen once before, something he couldn't describe. He walked up next to her, but at a distance, because he feared she would smell the meat on his breath, although he had brushed his teeth and eaten mints and even now had gum in his mouth. She stood in the moonlight, and he could see the white orbs of the moon, one in each of her eyes.

"I know it may seem silly to you," she said. "But it matters to me. As much as anything matters. Not only the way these animals are treated and slaughtered but the idea itself. The value. It's not a pretend value for me. It's not a hip issue. It's what I believe. And guess what?"

She turned to him. She looked at his belly.

"What is it?" he asked.

She stopped looking at his belly and looked at his face. "You know my *Meat Is Murder* series?" she asked.

"Yeah! It's fucking brilliant," he said.

"Well, a foundation made an offer."

"Really? How much?"

"Enough to buy this place, if we want."

They both screamed with excitement, like children, and she jumped into his arms and hugged him, and then she kissed him on the lips.

She suddenly pushed him away, put her hand over her mouth as if she were going to gag.

"What?"

"Really? Are you serious?" she said.

"What are you talking about?"

"Brush and floss and rinse then take a shower. And you better scrub hard, till your skin is red, because the smell of death comes out of your pores! ¡Cochino!"

In bed that night, she turned on her side, her back to him.

As he lay in the dark, he wondered if he still smelled like dead animal, like when their bodies are rotting in the sun. He imagined the stench coming from his mouth, his ears, his pores, out of his farts and sweat.

It was disgusting, the air thick with rotting flesh. He wanted to get up and put on a fan or open a window, and he wondered how she could sleep. Then he could taste it in his mouth, vomit and dead animal, and he tried not to, but he swallowed, and the poison made his eyes water.

# FUCK SHAKESPEARE

"Fuck Shakespeare!" Bino said.

He stood with his feet firmly on the ground, his shadow looming over me. Andrés had told me that Bino was a former Green Beret, a black belt who could kill with two fingers. Now he was a Chicano radical, an activist who used militant tactics.

"What do you like about him?" he asked, jerking his head up as if he were about to kill me.

I stuttered my answer: "A-a certain universality of . . ."

"Fuck him," he shot. "I hate that white asshole."

"Yeah, Bino prefers brown assholes," Andrés said.

Students walking along the path had to step on the lawn to get around us. Bino towered over me, and I shifted my feet wondering what he wanted from me, why he had stopped me as I was walking out of the library. He was a seventh-year sociology major. Some days in the free speech area he'd make impromptu diatribes against the university or the government. His words were so strong—"Reagan *is* the KKK!" he'd say, and he attracted crowds.

He was a favorite of the MEChistAs, but others didn't know how to handle him. They thought that they were entering a political debate in the free speech area, but he only let them talk for about five seconds before he went nuts, sticking his finger in their faces, calling them racists. He could rile up the radical Chicano students so it looked like they were about to start turning over cars and blowing up buildings. "Have you even taken a Shakespeare class?" I said to him, kind of snobbishly. I hadn't meant to sound that way, but I was just confident that he hadn't ever read Shakespeare.

"What the hell for?" he asked. "What does it matter to that Chicano kid who was beat up by those frat boys? Right here on campus? You heard about that? Happened here, a week ago. Or were you too busy reading *Romeo and Juliet?*"

"If you spics want to talk," Andrés said in a mock Okie accent, "you'd better do it on the grass. Decent white folks is using this path."

"We're reclaiming this land in the name of Aztlán," Bino said. "Them whiteys can go back to Europe."

I looked around, just to make sure no one had heard that. Although Andrés looked white—tall, dirty blond hair, blue eyes—he was dressed like a cholo, an urban Chicano gangbanger with creased Ben Davis work pants, an ironed white T-shirt, and black work boots. An unlit cigarette dangled from his lips as he patted his pockets for matches. "I mean, think about it, fellas," he whined like a bratty white boy. "You're holding up traffic."

"I have to go to class," I said.

"Shakespeare?" Bino asked, as if the thought made him sick.

"You know, there really is a lot to admire in his writings," I said. "One just has to put one's prejudices aside."

Bino stepped in closer to me. He put his face inches from mine, like an evil version of the cop in that Norman Rockwell painting. His teeth were clenched: "What? What the hell did he write that's so important to us?"

I could feel the heat of his breath on my face. I took a few steps back and looked to Andrés, who lit his cigarette, took a long drag, and blew the smoke into the air.

"Well, sheer volume alone is impressive," I said.

"Suppose he was several writers," Andrés said. "I read that somewhere. What if Shakespeare was a bunch of people?"

"That's stupid," I said.

"Why's it stupid?"

"Those theories have been discredited."

"Aha! But by who?"

*By whom*, I wanted to correct.

"By white people, ¿qué no?" Andrés continued. "Nobody would publish the truth."

"That doesn't even matter," Bino said, slinging the backpack over his other shoulder to free both hands, like a soldier ready for hand-to-hand combat. "The important question for our people," he said, "is what did Shakespeare, a white icon—What did Shakespeare, an example of the superior white mind—What did Shakespeare do for *our* people, *our* people who struggle every day?" He held up a finger as if it represented "our people."

"What does he mean to *our* people, our people who have a right to dignity but get none? What is to be admired in his works, not from a gabacho perspective but from a Chicano perspective?"

"Not a damn thing," said Andrés. "You're right about that, Bino."

"You guys are writers," Bino said. "What are you doing for the Movement? What are you doing for the people?" He looked at me. "I saw one of your poems in that English Department journal. It was about a stupid horse eating grass! What the fuck is that shit? You should be writing about the struggle." He stepped back and looked at both of us. "If you guys were down for the people, down for the revolution, you wouldn't care about getting published. You wouldn't care about the glory, the recognition, the pats on the back. You wouldn't care about the book contracts, the letter from Knopf saying you're the greatest writer they ever encountered so here's a thousand dollars for your next book. You wouldn't care about signing your name to what you've written. You'd all use the same name, one name."

He paused and ran a palm over his short hair. The sides were graying. He must have been about forty-five years old. "I write poetry," he said. "Did you know that? But I never sign my work. Oh, no. What I write is not, I repeat, *is not* Bino Duran emotionally masturbating on the page. It's the voice of the people crying out for justice."

"It wasn't really about a horse," I said. "That was a metaphor—"

"Fuck your metaphors! The poet is either a clown or an enemy of the oppressor. What we need—what our people need—is a Chicano Shakespeare, someone to speak out for our needs. One voice. We should put all our writings together and publish them under one name, one writer. The Writer."

"Hold on there, feller," Andrés said, in his Okie voice. "Now you're talking a little crazy-like. It's easy for you to give up your poems because you write shit. But when you're a genius like me . . ."

From some distance away, between two buildings, my eyes were pulled to Manuel Padilla walking toward the library. He was on time. My heart jumped because I didn't want him to see me next to these guys. I looked around as if I might find an escape but found instead my reflection in the mirrored windows of the library: a little dark boy, round face, thick black hair that looked greasy, dressed in dark slacks and a long-sleeved white shirt. I looked like a busboy.

"I have to go study," I said.

Both Andrés and Bino held out their hands for the Chicano hand-shake, each step of which was so awkward and slow for me. I submitted my thin fingers to their strong grips.

Manuel stood up at the head of the table, lecturing in front of four or five others, all of them holding pens, their books open. Across the hall, I sat at an oak table and tried to concentrate on reading *Hamlet*, but I couldn't stop looking at him. I imagined touching his face with the back of my fingers, and him looking up at me with eyes that sparkled love.

In reality, of course, he was taller than me and would have to look down to make eye contact; and he was untouchable to a guy like me. I wasn't even out, and I didn't feel like I could be because of Andrés and the other Chicanos. They may have thought themselves all progressive, but Andrés freely used the word "faggot" to describe people he didn't like.

Andrés was sitting across from me carving into the oak table with a pocketknife. "Hey look at this," he said. He had carved the *Lowrider* logo, the face of a mustached cholo. "Pretty cool, ¿qué no?"

Manuel put on a pair of glasses and read a passage from the book out loud to the others as he walked back and forth.

"Come outside with me while I smoke," Andrés said. He pulled out a cigarette.

I ignored him, ignored Shakespeare, watched Manuel, and there was a certain bend in his front lip, like the start of a smirk.

"Come on, man. Come smoke with me."

"I don't smoke," I said.

Andrés turned around to see what had me so absorbed. "Why you keep looking at Manuel Padilla like that? Got a crush on him, maricón?"

"Just go smoke," I said.

"Sellout," he said, but he just stood there, because he didn't like to smoke alone.

I looked down at the words of *Hamlet*, pretending to be absorbed, hoping Manuel would—at that moment—look over at me and see how hard I studied, hoping he would notice me, although I wasn't much to notice.

The youngest of ten boys, I was the shortest and darkest. They called me *El Indio*. They all still lived in Farmersville, working the nearby almond fields or as forklift drivers. Although one other brother finished high school, I was the only one to go to college.

Now I scratched my head, as if the passage I read, because it was so complex, required extra thought.

"I wonder what he's doing with all those white people," Andrés said.

"It's a study group," I said.

"Dude, why do you look at him like that?"

"Like what?" I asked. "He's interesting. That's all."

"He's not a fag."

"You shouldn't use that word," I said.

"Come on, sellout! Come outside with me so I can smoke." He stood up, expecting me to do the same.

"I'm not a sellout," I said.

"Come with me," he said, stressing "me" with a whine. "Do it for the people."

"Just because I don't hate white people doesn't mean I'm a sellout," I said. "If I did, I'd have to hate you, Okie."

"Only half of me," he said. "I'm a Chicanokie."

While one of his hands held his eyeglasses, Manuel used the other to emphasize a point he was making. That almost smirk on his upper lip.

"Come on, man," said Andrés, a cigarette in his lips. "Let's go."

"I'm studying," I said. "Go yourself."

"You're acting like a white boy," he said. "Like that boy." He pulled the cigarette from his lips and pointed with it.

I turned around and saw Stanley Monk, president of the campus Greens, walking toward us, his smile growing big with recognition.

"I hate that gabacho," Andrés said.

"Is that why you're always drinking beer together?" I asked.

"Shit, he pays for it," said Andrés.

"What are you guys doing?" Stanley asked, as if we were his best friends. His skin was much darker than usual because he had spent the summer at the beach. His curly blond hair made him look like a photo negative.

"I'm trying to study," I said.

He looked down at my book and his eyes widened. "Shakespeare. Have you been to the English Department?"

"It's my day off," I said. "Why?"

"Someone spray-painted all over the walls, all over the walls in big letters. You know what they wrote?" Stanley asked.

"Just fucking tell us," snapped Andrés.

"Fuck Shakespeare."

I looked at Andrés, who looked at me.

"It's everywhere," Stanley continued. "'Fuck Shakespeare' all over the place. It's hilarious."

"Hur! Hur! Hur!" said Andrés, making fun of how white people laugh.

"Andrés, did you know about this?" I asked.

"Not me," he said.

"Who do you think did it?" Stanley asked.

"How the fuck would we know?" Andrés asked, stepping in like he was ready to fight.

"Don't get offended. I'm just asking."

"You're just assuming that since it's graffiti it was done by a Chicano," said Andrés.

"You guys are too paranoid," Stanley said.

"*You* guys? I didn't even say anything," I said.

"He means Mexicans," said Andrés. "He's racist. Just like the rest of them."

"Give me a break," Stanley said, as if trying not to take Andrés seriously. He took the backpack from his shoulder and placed it on the table. He sat across from me and looked in my eyes. "You know I didn't mean that."

"What *did* you mean?" asked Andrés.

"I'm ignoring you," he said to Andrés. Then to me: "Personally, I think it was Brad Jenkins. He flunked Shakespeare. Now he can't graduate. He's real pissed because he wanted to teach English in Japan. Had it all planned."

Manuel sat down and listened to someone else in his study group talk, some white guy who looked like a frat boy, clean-cut, handsome, white teeth. After he was done, everyone in the study group began to close their books. Manuel took off his glasses and began to put his stuff away. To get out, he would have to walk right by us.

While Stanley and Andrés went on talking, he passed by, holding his briefcase, walking very professionally toward the elevator. He said hello to Andrés, who said hi back, and then Stanley said, "Hiya, Manuel," and waved.

"Hello, Stanley," he said.

Then he looked right at me and raised his eyebrows as if to say, "That Stanley guy's a loser," as if there were a joke between us. When he reached the elevator, he pressed the button and then turned around, facing us as he waited.

"You know what your problem is?" I said to Stanley. "You think you're so liberal because you care about trees and toxic waste and you vote with the Greens, but you don't give a damn about Chicanos. You and your causes—your anti–nuclear power demonstrations—are just a bunch of bourgeois games that do nothing more than mitigate your guilt for being so rich and privileged."

I could tell by the way Manuel took a step closer to us that I had his attention. Andrés's mouth dropped opened as he watched me go on.

"What have the Greens ever done for us?" I continued, hoping the elevator would come soon because I really wasn't sure where I was going with this. I imagined I was Bino giving a speech. "Over 50 percent of our children never graduate high school. What do you guys care? Most of our people are in poverty. What do you guys care?"

"Hey! We are actively recruiting Chicanos to join the Greens!" he said.

"To join *your* fight," I said. "To join your bourgeois fight. What about when a Chicano kid is beat up by frat boys? They called him 'greaser' and 'spic.' Where were the Greens then?"

I wanted to ask what the Greens had ever done for gays, but I just stopped. Stanley stood. "You guys are unreasonable. I'll see you later."

"Who's 'you guys'?" I asked.

He waved off my question with one arm.

"Hey, Stanley," Andrés yelled.

Stanley turned around, hands on his hips.

"What?" he asked.

"Fuck Shakespeare," said Andrés.

We laughed.

Like a proud father Andrés looked at me. "That was great. What happened, man? I mean, what got into you, ese?"

Manuel's elevator arrived and he stepped in, but before the door closed he smiled at me. There was no question he was gay. I knew it. I knew it.

Then the administration building—an old brick structure nestled on the lawn between two more modern buildings—was splattered in white paint, letters big as humans, "Fuck Shakespeare." The line of oak trees outside the library had a red letter painted on each trunk. On one side of the path were the letters FUCKSHAK, and on the other were ESPEARE. The graffiti was signed *El Escritor*.

Then things got ugly.

Most of the books in the library by or about Shakespeare were destroyed—pages torn, passages crossed out with black markers, and the covers sliced with a knife. *El Escritor* didn't claim this work—nor the black ink poured over the brand-new stack of collected works in the bookstore—but everyone assumed it was *El Escritor* and that he was a Chicano, especially after one wall was painted with "Chúpame Chakespeare."

As I was making copies one morning in the English Department where I worked assisting the secretaries, I heard a couple of English professors talking about the graffiti.

"It's a misdirected form of protest. It's certainly not in the spirit of César Chávez, whom I met once. I think a boycott or a march would have been much more effective."

"Oh, I agree," said the other.

They came into the copy room, Karen and Mike, which is how they liked to be called by their students, and they both looked at me and stopped, as if they were surprised to find me making copies.

"Hi," I finally said. They looked at each other as if wondering if they should ask. Finally, Karen hooked her long, thin blonde hair behind her ears. "Can we ask you something?"

I stood frozen, the machine spitting out copies *chinga chinga chinga*. "Sure. Why not? What is it?"

*Chinga chinga chinga*

As if on cue, they took two steps closer and then looked at each other and behind them to make sure no one was coming.

Finally Karen spoke. "Who's doing the tagging?"

"What?" I asked.

"It's cool," assured Mike, pushing his glasses up his nose. "We understand. I mean, we were around in the '60s."

"As students," Karen clarified.

*Chinga chinga chinga*

"We believe that it's a form of, well . . ."

"Political expression," Karen finished.

"Yeah, man, and we understand that, believe me. We've been there."

"I was maced by the police in Berkeley," Karen said proudly.

"I was, well, I was involved in a lot of crazy stuff," said Mike.

The copy machine stopped and the silence buzzed. The two secretaries in the outer office were pretending not to be looking at us as they sat at their desks thumbing through papers.

"I'm not sure what you want me to say," I said.

"*El Escritor*," Mike said, as if the words were significant. He might have even winked at me.

"What?" I said.

"Never mind," Karen said, leading Mike out of the copy room.

I finished the copies and walked into the main office where the two secretaries sat at their desks. Dr. Dart, the English Department chair, stood in his doorframe shaking his head. He was a little man, my size, with a beard like a rabbi's. "Stupid," he said. "It's stupid."

And he closed his door.

Later, I thought how strange it was that I had never been involved in anything Chicano, the organizations, protests, nothing, yet many people assumed I was connected to *El Escritor*, connected to the Chicano students. Maybe it was because Andrés was my roommate. Maybe it was my complexion, the Indianness of my nose.

One afternoon as I walked through campus, I saw Bino sitting with Manuel Padilla and a woman I didn't know. They were outside the cafeteria at a group of tables students referred to as "Little Tijuana" because so many Chicanos sat around there. I had never hung out there myself because I didn't know many people except for Andrés, but Bino saw me and waved me over.

"It's *El Escritor*," he said as I walked over.

Chicanos at other tables looked at me. Bino stood up to offer me his hand, as if I were someone important. I went through the steps of the handshake, dreading the end, because there were women there too, and I wasn't sure if I should do it with them. I had never seen Chicano men shake hands with Chicana women the same way they did with other men, and it always seemed sexist not to. But I couldn't NOT treat the woman the same way, but still, after Bino let go of my hand, I withdrew it. I didn't offer it to anyone else.

"*El Escritor*," the woman said to me. "What's next on your agenda?"

"I don't know," I said. "Ask Bino."

"Sit down," Bino said.

He had a copy of the campus newspaper, and the front-page head-line read: "Bard Hater Terrorizes Campus." I could make out in the first paragraph that *El Escritor* had threatened to blow up the theater where a production of *Richard III* was being rehearsed. The tires were slashed and the windows busted out on the director's car. I looked at Manuel's wrist, his watch. It was sleek, with golden roman numerals for the hours.

"The chair of the English Department thinks I'm responsible," I said. "I guess it's because I'm Hispanic. I mean, Chicano."

Manuel put down the paper and put his elbows on the table as if ready to hear a good story. "What did he say?" he asked.

"It's just the way he acts."

"You're an English major, right?" he asked.

I admitted I was.

"Andrés was telling me about you. He says you're pretty smart." My heart started to beat so hard that I was afraid he would hear it.

Make no mistake, this is a love story.

I looked at his wristwatch because I couldn't look in his eyes for very long. "You're the chair of Chicanos in Law, right?" I asked.

"Yeah, how come you don't come to our meetings? We could use a good writer."

"We can always use *El Escritor*," said Bino.

I looked around, hoping no one was paying attention. "People might really think I'm him," I whispered.

"What do you mean 'Think'?" he said, loudly, standing up. "You mean they KNOW who is *El Escritor*."

Bino and the woman went and sat with a group of Chicano students at another table and started talking with them, leaving me alone with Manuel. My palms started to sweat.

When I looked over at him, I found that he had been watching me, his eyes gentle.

I was happy.

Finally I stammered and stuttered what came to me: "Can I see your watch?"

He held out his wrist. There was a black leather band with something engraved in it, a name, although it didn't look like "Manuel."

"It's nice," I said.

"I liked what you were saying the other day to Stanley Monk," he said. "Someone who can speak the way you can needs to be involved," he said. "You should write something for us."

"Sure, of course. Like a poem?"

"An article explaining the graffiti," he said.

"I'm not sure I understand it myself. I have nothing against Shakespeare," I said.

"This has nothing to do with Shakespeare," he said. "I understand he was a great writer. But this is a vehicle for mobilization. People are paying attention."

"I tend to stay neutral as much as possible," I said, stuttering the "N" on neutral for about seven beats.

"Neutral?" he said, as if the thought were disgusting. "What does 'neutral' mean? And don't define it according to Webster. What does it mean politically? Compliance? Acceptance of the status quo? There is no such thing as neutrality. That's a bourgeois concept."

"What do you even mean by bourgeois?" I asked. "You sound like robots."

"Oh, my God, I can't believe you're serious," he said.

"Never mind, I just . . . you see why I don't like to talk politics? It's too divisive. Can we change the subject? Tell me about you."

He sat there looking at me, shaking his head, as if he hated what he saw. "No, I don't think so," he said.

"I have to go," I said, and without looking at him I rose from my seat and walked away. I know I looked funny, my arms swinging from side to side as if I had no elbows, but I kept walking away until I lost all consciousness and my body took over.

I went to the English Department for work, and when I walked in, I noticed the secretaries looked nervous. I stood before their desks and asked what I should do. Then I heard a crash come from Dr. Dart's office, and I heard him cuss.

"His car was vandalized," one of the women explained.

The office, quiet most of the day, had an oppressive air about it, and everyone whispered. When I finished making a stack of copies, I brought it to the secretary and she told me to take it to Dr. Dart.

I knocked on the door. "What?"

"I have some papers for you," I said.

"Well come in then," he snapped.

When I opened the door, the papers slipped from my grip and flew all over the floor.

"What are you doing?" he yelled, standing up. He was such a tiny man that we were almost eye-to-eye.

"I'm sorry, Dr. Dart—" I bent down to pick them up.

"Just leave," he said, "I'll get them."

I stood up and stumbled into a wooden coatrack, knocking it down. With a thud it hit his desk. I apologized.

"Just . . . leave," Dart said, trying to contain his anger.

I kept apologizing, gathering papers from the floor and dropping them again, making a greater mess. As he continued to tell me to leave, I ceased to hear words, just saw his mouth moving in slow motion.

And I realized.

I was doing this on purpose.

When he slammed the door behind me, I felt pretty good. I turned around, and the secretaries were looking at me. "I think I should take the rest of the day off," I said. They nodded agreement.

A cool breeze swept through the pines that surrounded our balcony. Andrés and I had bought beer and tri tip. I unrolled the end of the stiff, hard charcoal bag, poured the chunks into the barbecue, squeezed on the lighter fluid, and let it soak. The sharp gas smell gave me a headache. Inside, Andrés was singing along with his favorite Led Zeppelin tape, his screeching voice like a wail of anguish.

*When you feeeeeeeeel like you can't go on*

In the metal black bowl where the charcoal was piled I saw Dr. Dart yelling, spittle dripping from his beard. I saw Manuel shaking his head at me. I saw Bino's face scrunched up in anger, pointing his finger.

The doorbell rang and Andrés went to answer it. "Well I'll be a monkey's uncle!" he exclaimed in his best Okie accent.

Through the glass I saw Stanley Monk. "Look what I brought for us, my friends," he said as he walked out on the balcony and ceremoniously pulled from a paper sack a six-pack of foreign beer in green bottles.

"What the hell kind of beer is that?" Andrés asked.

"This, gentlemen, is the best beer your ugly asses will ever drink." He opened one and handed it to Andrés.

"What the hell," Andrés said, gulping the bottle of Bud he already had and then taking a swig of the new one. "Hey, not bad."

"The best," Stanley said, handing one to me.

"No thanks," I said. "I'm still on my first."

"Come on," he urged. "Try a real beer."

"Later," I said.

"I'll put this in the refrigerator," he said, entering the apartment, singing along with the music. "I didn't know Chicanos listened to

Zeppelin," he yelled. The phone rang and Stanley answered it. When he came out he said, "There's some señora on the phone speaking Spanish."

"My mom," I said. "I'm going to turn the music down," I told Andrés.

"Hell no, you ain't," Andrés said. He had glassy eyes, which meant he was getting drunk.

"Well, then, I'm taking the call in your room."

I went inside and told my mom I'd call her back, so she wouldn't have to pay for it. I walked down the hall.

I reached his door.

When I opened it, cold air and a flood of nervousness washed over me. Things looked normal enough: papers and books were scattered everywhere, even on the floor surrounding the wooden legs of the desk, as if Andrés had been looking for something by throwing stuff around until he had found it. The walls were lined on three sides by bookshelves—thick tomes on politics and revolution—and they made the room feel small, almost confining, like an interrogation cell. On the wall hung a Malaquias Montoya poster of an illegal Mexican wrapped and suffocating in an American flag, and next to that was a life-sized poster of Zapata staring in my eyes as he held his rifle. The computer and the telephone were on the desk. I nervously sat, feeling as if I were being watched, and called my mom.

My father was getting more senile, she said. I pictured him sitting, not at home in his regular recliner but across Andrés's room on the futon, scratching his disheveled white hair, mouth moving as if chewing without teeth, and looking around, clueless about where he was.

My oldest brother, Miguel, she added, had lost his job because the farm had been sold. He and his wife were having hard times.

She said I should write something nice for him, perhaps a poem, forgetting that he couldn't read English and I couldn't write Spanish. "Write down with pen and paper," she said slowly, "the new address of your brother."

I placed one hand on the desk top, on the scattered papers, and felt for a pen.

My face froze in disgust as I felt around in the mess, because I almost expected to be bitten by something. I grabbed a piece of paper and wrote the address in my large, childlike handwriting. We said our good-byes. I hung up. I looked at the address.

The piece of paper had been torn from a Shakespeare book.

I had to admit to myself what I had already sensed. Andrés was *El Escritor*.

He had been a member of MEChistA ever since I met him and was good at putting across the radical rhetoric of Bino, but inside he was still a kid. I once saw him get excited when the waitress at Denny's accidentally brought a kid's menu to our table along with some crayons. He sat there the entire time coloring the faces, holding the paper up for me to see, saying, "Now that's talent!"

Perhaps Bino didn't take him seriously, and this was a way of doing his part, although I wasn't sure what it had accomplished or why they embraced it as a revolutionary action. Perhaps the publicity.

Out the window, I saw Andrés squatting in front of the barbecue eating beef slices off the grill with one hand while holding a cigarette with the other. He pulled off a strip and handed it to Stanley, a vegetarian, who put his hand over his mouth as if gagging. Andrés shrugged his shoulders, gobbled up the meat, took a drink of beer and a drag off his cigarette.

"Hey, Andrés," I yelled out the window. "Come here for a second."

"You come here, shit," he said. He was drunk.

"Seriously. I gotta tell you something."

"Fuck," he said, raising his beer to his mouth as he felt his way into the apartment. He came in the room. "This better be good."

"What's this?" I asked, holding out the page.

"Looks like an address," he said.

"I mean, what is it written on?"

He examined it closely. "Looks like a page from *Romeo and Juliet*," he said, shaking his beer bottle to see how much was left. "So, what do you want?"

"You're *El Escritor!*" I said. "Why didn't you tell me?"

"What the fuck are you talking about?"

"You're *El Escritor*. You've been doing all that damage. How come you never told me? I was sure it was Bino."

Andrés looked at me in disbelief, and since he was drunk, his expression was exaggerated, like he thought I was the biggest idiot in the world. "Man," he exclaimed, "you're really stupid. I can't believe how stupid you are. No wonder nobody likes you."

"What are you getting upset about?"

"I had hope for you, man, but you're just a little tío taco who don't know shit. All your life you try to fit in with the gabachos, but you're too damn brown to ever do that. It don't matter what you think of yourself, white people see you coming and they see a little brown Indian, a little *mojado*. But you're too stupid to realize it. All you've managed to achieve is making your own people hate you."

"What the hell are you talking about?" I yelled. "Who hates me?"

"Wake up and smell the frijoles, coconut."

"You know, the heck with you!" I yelled, storming out of his room and into mine. I slammed the door shut.

"Man, you are stupid," I could hear Andrés say.

A little later I heard a knock on my door. I stood up from my bed and went to answer it, expecting it to be Andrés ready to apologize, but it was Stanley, standing there shaking his head.

"What do you want?" I said.

"Andrés says you didn't know. Is that true? You didn't know?"

"Know what? You mean, who *El Escritor* is? Well I found . . ."

"*El Escritor* is everybody," he said. "Even me. I even did some of the spray paint."

"You're *El Escritor*?"

"No, not me. Everybody. I did my part just to show my support. Although personally I think there are other channels. *El Escritor* isn't one person. It's the Chicanos, man. How could you not know that? I'm not a Chicano, and even I knew it."

"Then why did you act innocent that day in the library?" I asked.

"Even Andrés didn't know about it then."

I pictured this: Andrés tearing pages out of library books, slashing the covers with his pocketknife, slashing the tires of the director's car; Bino writing the giant letters on the trees; Manuel's wrist twisting, the watch sparkling against the black ink that poured slowly like oil over the books. No wonder he thought I was such an idiot to deny that *El Escritor* was me. How could I have been so out of touch? How could I have been so separated from everyone else? *El Escritor* was not one writer but a bunch of them, under one name.

Now I was standing alone in a dark hallway at the university, watching a figure walking toward me from the hallway lined by numbered doors. I knew it was Bino.

On the walls close to where I stood were freshly painted words: "Fuck Shakespeare" and "Queers hate the Bard."

Bino stepped closer to me and stopped. He looked at the red words dripping on the walls. He extended his arms as if wind blew through him. "This is great," he said. "What's that you got there?" he asked, indicating my hand, which I held behind my back.

I showed him the can of spray paint. "I, uh, found it in the trash," I said. "*El Escritor* must have just left."

Bino let out a hearty laugh like a lumberjack. "Probably he ran when he saw you coming."

"It wasn't me," I said.

"Get rid of that can," he said. I tossed it in the trash.

We walked out together, into the night, bushes and trees going wild in the wind. The air was cool.

"You know," Bino said, stopping to look at me. "Your fight is important too. I know we need to be more open, more inclusive. We haven't been good at that, and I'm sorry. Things are changing, man. You could help with that."

"What can I do?" I asked.

"Come with me," he said. "Let's meet with some of the MEChistAs."

"Sure," I said.

We walked through the double doors of the well-lit campus coffee shop, and across the vast floor I saw Andrés and a woman at a table.

When we arrived at the table, and I offered Andrés the Chicano handshake. Then I offered my hand to the woman. She firmly grasped mine, and we went through the Chicano handshake together, step by step.

# A HOUSE OF THEIR OWN

They bought the house with beautiful city views all the way to the mountains. She wondered if it was too expensive, but he assured her it would work.

One morning, he woke up, hungover, to the noise of tractors and hammers and drills. He looked out the window and saw a line of white trucks and an army of men working in yellow hardhats.

They learned it would be a high school, three stories high, two blocks wide. It would block their view and put them in shadow.

After the divorce, they sold the house at a great loss. She left the country, and he moved in with his mother.

# LADY OF THE SILVER LAKE

He loved the movies, and on his way to Oaxaca he had to transfer planes in LA, so why not stay two days and see Hollywood? He wanted to stick his hands in the cement prints left by great stars like David Hasselhoff. He had heard so many stories about Hollywood that he was certain if he just walked around for the day he would see a movie star.

The afternoon found him in front of Grauman's Chinese theater. There were no movie stars, but there were out-of-work actors poorly dressed like superheroes. There was a skinny Incredible Hulk, his fake biceps sliding off his arms, and he saw a skinny Spiderman slip into the alley to smoke a cigarette, his mask pulled off a face so skeletal he must have been a drug addict. He saw Superman, circus-tall and skinny with a potbelly, and the only thing Superman-y about him was a cowlick, heavy with gel, curling over one eye.

After a full day looking for stars, he only wanted to find where he had parked his car. It was a rental, and he forgot what the color was—*red? blue? white?*—so he walked for hours looking for it.

He stepped into a coffee shop to use their toilet, but it was locked, so he went up to ask for the key. That was when he saw the two young Mexican women who worked there. They were behind the counter, talking to each other in Spanish. As he approached, he tried to see if he could understand what they were saying. One was telling the other about the lousy date she had had the night before, a real jerk, she was saying. She had long black hair that made her look very Mexican, he noticed.

He pictured her in a long Mexican dress, embroidered at the hem, and a red flower in her hair.

She was a classic Mexican beauty, he thought, a dignified Roman nose, a beauty mark on her upper lip, and such big, dark eyes! She turned toward him and asked, What can I get you?

He spoke in Spanish. Está cerrado el WC.

I speak English, she said.

I don't to speak good English. I sorry, he said.

She looked at him amused.

He was dressed in short cargo pants with lots of pockets, and he wore tennis shoes with white socks pulled up to below his knees and a V-neck sweater. He was tall and thin and wore glasses, and thanks to his height, not many people noticed his bald spot. She was much shorter than him, coming to his chest.

Where are you from? she asked.

Lo siento, pero no entiendo, he said.

¿De donde eres?

Rusia, he answered.

¿Pero hablas español?

¡Claro que sí!

She smiled at him, and her eyes seemed to take on a different shape, like a cat, an ocelot, or a leopard, like she had cornered him and was about to attack. Tienes que ordenar algo, si quieres usar el baño.

¿Me daría un cafecito? por favor.

Claro, was all she said. She turned around and got the cup. She turned to say something to him, looked over her shoulder like a 1940s American pinup model. She cleared her throat and she asked, Room for cream?

His face was red.

She had to think about how to say it in Spanish. Espacio para la crema? Or no . . . para leche. ¿Quieres leche en tu café?

No, gracias, negro. Puro negro.

Instead of taking his coffee to go, he drank it there. He sat near enough so that he could watch her and hear her conversion with the other. He tried to occasionally catch her eyes, and when he did, he smiled and raised his coffee cup, as if to say it was delicious. She walked over to his table. ¿Todo está bien?

Estoy cansado. Caminé mucho.

Yeah?

¿Dónde soy?

The Heavenly Bean, she said.

No, ¿quel parte de la ciudad?

Silver Lake, she said.

The silver lake? he repeated.

Just Silver Lake, she said. No *the.*

He asked her where was the best place to see movie stars, and she said you see them at the most unexpected places, in line at Target, walking out of a restaurant, anywhere, anytime. Try the Whole Foods in West Hollywood.

He asked other questions, until finally she laughed and said, You are a little lost one, aren't you?

He shrugged his shoulders.

¿Puedes enseñarme tu ciudad? he asked.

¿Cómo te llamas? she asked.

Misha, he said.

Misha? she asked.

He hoped she was flirting with him.

¿Puedes? he asked.

¿Cuánto tiempo estás aqui?

The lie just came out: Un mes, he said. Then after a month he would be going to Mexico, he told her.

Mexico? she asked.

He told her he would go to Oaxaca and asked if she knew what it was like there.

I've been to Tijuana, she said. And Rosarito Beach. We got trashed.

He asked again if she could show him around town.

She smiled and told him okay, but not until the day after tomorrow. She gave him the address and told him to pick her up at five p.m.

As he drove back to the hotel, he imagined that they would become passionate about each other, and he pictured them saying good-bye at the airport. She's crying, pleading for him to come back.

Of course! Of course I will!

But, sadly, he never would come back to LA.

Soon he'd have to go back to his small town and work at the hotel.

Then he remembered that his flight left the morning of their date. I can't believe it, he said to himself. He was stopped at a red light, and he put his head on the steering wheel and rocked it back and forth mumbling, No, no, no, until the cars behind him started honking. Some people yelled out their windows for him to move it. He looked up and saw that the light was green.

When he got back to the hotel, he thought that maybe he could show up a day early and feign like he had gotten the day wrong, and maybe she would go out with him anyway. Or maybe he could call her and ask if they could move the day up, say that he had a business meeting or something. He pulled the little piece of paper out of his wallet.

He picked up the phone and was about to call her when he noticed that she hadn't written down her phone number, just her address, and he realized he didn't even ask for her name.

He was depressed.

He lay in the bed and turned on the TV. He flicked through the channels. Many of them were in Spanish, but there didn't seem to be much on. He couldn't stop thinking about the lady in the silver lake. Why couldn't two different people from two different parts of the world fall in love with each other? It had happened before. He fell asleep picturing her smile.

He was on a bus with a bunch of people, going somewhere, but as they passed a little farm he realized that he was supposed to be at that farm. There was a party and he was supposed to meet everyone in the barn. In the front of the well, his dog, dead ten years, was sitting in the tall grass, as if waiting for him. He yelled the dog's name out the window of the bus, and the dog, hearing his name, looked up and around. He yelled for the bus driver to pull over, but the bus kept going.

The next day he tried to find the café in the silver lake, so he could ask her to change the day, but he couldn't find it and ended up back in Hollywood. He parked and started walking down Hollywood Boulevard, trying to retrace his steps. He had to stop to wait for a group of German tourists to take pictures of the stupid-looking

Spiderman. After they moved on and were out of sight, the Spiderman came up to him and said, I don't get paid.

Misha smiled and tried to walk on, but Spiderman stepped in front of him, put his face inches from his. He smelled like cigarettes and booze.

I'm not legally allowed to ask for tips, he said, but you guys took a lot of fucking pictures.

I'm not with them, he said, aware of his own accent. I'm Russian.

Right, said, Spiderman, nodding. Then he leaned in even closer. Look, der Führer. You better the fuck give me something.

It cost him a painful 250 dollars, about 1,400 rubles, but he changed his flight and gave himself a few extra days in LA. He GPSed her address and found it was in East LA, so he Googled that and read a little about the area. According to some descriptions, it was like Mexico, the population, the markets, and it was also one of the oldest parts of the city. He read that it even had its own walk of fame, just like the one in Hollywood, only for Latino stars, the Latino Walk of Fame, they called it.

That afternoon he stood in front of the concierge's desk to ask about the best way to get to East LA.

The concierge, an old man, said, East LA? Why do you want to go there?

To meet a lady, he said.

Are you sure you want to go there?

Why wouldn't I?

The concierge looked around, as if to see if anyone was listening, then he leaned over his desktop toward the stranger. Chicano gangs, he said.

Chicano?

Yeah, you know? Hispanics gone bad. Chicanos are like Mexicans with an attitude. They're bad news, my friend. There's some mean cholos over there.

Cholos?

Bato locos, he said. They'll kill you as easy as smile at you. It's not safe. I wouldn't recommend going.

He went back to his room and Googled Chicano gangs. Apparently, there were a lot of Chicanos in East LA, and they seemed to be of

Mexican origin but they didn't seem to be Mexican. They carried guns and fought a lot and killed a lot, just like the concierge had said. He read about a twelve-year-old boy who had been shot ten times and whose mother was shot in the face. He remembered his own mother, an involuntary image of her sticking her head out the window of their second-story apartment yelling down to him with a desperate voice, Don't come home yet, Misha. Go play.

He Google-image-searched "Chicano" and "cholo" and saw how they dressed differently from Mexicans, like they were some secret society with rules and hierarchies, and some social code only they seemed to know about. One description compared them to armies, soldiers who had to obey the will of the leadership. He Google-image-searched "chola," the female version, and he saw images of young Mexican women (well, Chicanas) who looked as tough as the men. He watched homemade gang videos on YouTube, tough-looking Chicano boys and Chicana girls holding guns.

He remembered the lady's smile.

She was a nice girl, and he wanted to see her.

So he got into the rental car and drove to East LA. He found her house among a group of bungalows, and he parked the car in front on the street.

There were a few "cholos" hanging out in front of the complex, teenage boys with nothing to do. One of them was squatting against the wall, cholo style, just like Misha had seen in the Google image search. They watched him park. He looked out the window, hoping to see the number of her bungalow from the car, hoping they wouldn't keep looking at him, but they did. He saw her bungalow number, the number 13, and he saw white curtains in the window. He got out. He made sure the car was locked and walked up to the door. He could hear the television. He knocked.

He heard a man's voice yell, Who is it? as if angry for the intrusion.

It's me, he said. He almost whispered it, high pitched, like a mouse. He cleared his voice and said like a man, I'm here to see the lady of the silver lake.

The door opened, and a big Chicano stood in the doorway. He wore a tank top undershirt and he had big arms with tattoos. What you want? he asked.

I'm here for the lady, he said.

My sister? Who are you?

He stepped forward, and the stranger stepped back. The tattoo on one of his arms had an image of a chola.

Behave, Nacho! she yelled from within the house. Come in Misha, she yelled. I'll be right out.

Misha? The brother repeated. Why you got a girl's name?

Let him in, Nacho!

The brother left the door open and walked away. He sat on the couch in front of the TV. Misha walked in. The couch was covered in a Mexican blanket, multicolored and bright. The furnishings were red and velvety, and in one corner of the room was an old console stereo that seemed to be unused, just a place to put stuff, like a big statue of an Aztec warrior holding a spear. Above that on the wall was a kitschy painting of a bullfight, the matador sticking a spear into the side of the bull. On another wall was a poster print of Monet's *Water Lilies* in a frame. The TV looked new, a flat-screen HDTV. The brother was playing some sort of video game that had his avatar running through a city with a gun. He went up to some man in a car, shot him, blood splattering, and then got into the car.

The brother looked toward the stranger as he maneuvered the controller. Where you from, bro? His shoulders moved up and down as he played.

Misha answered in Spanish, Soy de Rusia.

Why don't you speak English to me? the boy asked, as if offended.

The avatar shot some lady who was crossing the street. Smoked you! Nacho said.

I don't speak good English, he answered.

Damn, said the boy shaking his head. You're fresh off the boat. You ever been to the barrio?

He shook his head.

Well, you must be pretty damn brave wearing that. That's all I got to say.

Wearing what?

That T-shirt. I hope you're packing.

Packing?

You know, armed and dangerous. Wearing *that* T-shirt.

Misha looked down at his T-shirt. I don't understand.

It's red, dogg. You don't wear those colors in this barrio.

It's just a T-shirt.

The boy shook his head in disbelief. Man, you don't know nothing. I guarantee, some of the homeboys see you wearing those colors they'll smoke you.

Smoke me?

Like a Cuban.

I don't . . .

Hey, you ever played Grand Theft Auto? I got the X-rated version.

Indeed, the avatar was watching a hooker take off her clothes. The Chicano paused the game and turned around. It's like all you got to do, bro, is suspend disbelief. That's it. It's like you're really there, killing all those people, pounding all that ass.

The lady came out of the back. She looked stunning, a white skirt, a blue top, her hair freshly washed and wavy. She smelled fresh, like shampoo. Her lips looked full and red, and Misha forgot about everything. He just looked at her, stunned.

Misha! she said.

He wanted to say her name, but he didn't know it and it seemed too late to ask her what it was.

So he said, ¡Aquí estoy!

She stepped close to him and kissed him on the cheek. Her brother shook his head, as if he thought she was being stupid, but he didn't go back to his video game. He sat there and watched them, like they were a TV show.

What were you saying to him? she asked Nacho.

Just telling my new homie a bit about the barrio.

You are a living stereotype, she said. Then to Misha she said, Don't listen to him.

You look very nice, he said.

Let's go, she said.

As they walked out the door, Nacho said to him, You're a brave man, bro. He indicated his T-shirt. Know what I'm saying?

He opened the car door for her and waited for her to get in before he closed it. He got in the other side.

Let's start off with Venice Beach, she said. Have you been there?

No, he said, and they were off.

He was happy. On the way over there she pointed out some buildings. That's Cal State LA, she said. I study there.

What do you study? he asked.

Literature. What do you do in Russia, anyway?

What do I do in Russia?

Yeah, what kind of work.

Work? I . . . uh, I . . . work with people.

Like public relations?

Yes, like that.

I thought you said your English isn't very good.

I'm sorry?

We've been speaking English the whole time, Misha.

Es que tengo verguenza. Me siento más seguro en español.

She nodded her head. Listen, she said, in English. She turned her body in his direction, as if she was going to say something revealing. I know you're not trying to offend me. You're a nice guy, but I'd appreciate it if you didn't hold open the car door for me until I sit down. I mean, if you want to open it for me, that's fine, I do that for my friends. But don't wait for me to be seated and then close the door for me. You know what I mean?

What do you mean?

Just treat me like a friend, she said.

Venice Beach was a carnival, street performers, hippies, surfers, a muscular man in tight panties playing with silver globes, a man who walked on glass, young boys who did break-dancing, an old man who sat on a bench, a bucket in front of him, and every now and then he would yell, PUT SOME MONEY IN THE BUCKET!

A blonde lady stood outside a shop and yelled, Get your medical marijuana! Doctor on the premises! Get some in minutes!

There was on outdoor gym, muscle men lifting weights in the sand, and there was a basketball court with tough-looking guys running back and forth dribbling the ball, making shots like professional players. It was like the movies, and Misha was like a child walking through the set. His eyes were wide at all he saw. They passed a bunch of cholo boys, obviously gang members with tattoos on their necks and arms. He looked down on his red T-shirt and wondered if they would notice. When he passed by them, he moved away as far as he could.

I would like to buy a T-shirt, he said.

Sure, but first, let's eat.

They sat at an outdoor restaurant where a stream of people passed by, women in bikinis on skates, Jews with skullcaps, kids who looked all hip-hop and cool. Across from where they sat, a man was banging a jazz tune on a piano on the grass. In the background, there were tall palm trees and the blue reach of the ocean. He had seen this day so many times in the movies, but now the story was about the lady and him. He held her hands across the table and squeezed them. Thank you so much for showing me this place.

She gave his hands a quick squeeze as she said, You're welcome. Then she put her hands under the table, on her lap.

What struck him most were the waiters. Boys and girls in their twenties, friendly and good-looking, like characters in a sitcom. When they took the orders, they made a few jokes, as if everyone was their friend, and sometimes they would even slap you on the shoulder like a pal. They also moved fast. They put down the food, and right when it seemed like you were done eating—even if there was still food on your plate—they came by and grabbed the plate and put down the check. In the hotel back home, he would be scolded if he waited on tables like that.

You like stargazing? she asked. Look who's here.

Walking down the boardwalk was a man with gold chains and a silky white sweat suit zipped down to the muscular chest. He wore shiny white tennis shoes and walked with his big white dog, who had a diamond collar and fur as fine as a mink coat. People got out of his way to watch him walk by, his head up, proud, his dog's head up, proud, as if they were used to being looked at. Some people took pictures.

That's José Canseco, she said. You know, the baseball player?

Yes, yes, said, Misha. He's famous, yes? Is he on the Latino Walk of Fame?

I don't think so, she said.

Is he a Mexican?

No, he's from Cuba, I think.

What does it mean to smoke someone like a Cuban?

She laughed. Where did you hear that?

He shrugged his shoulders.

It's an expression. To smoke someone means to shoot him and kill him. And like a Cuban refers to the cigars. You know, Cuban cigars?

He leaned over the table to whisper something to her.

I must ask you something but please don't be offended.

She nodded.

Is your brother a . . . Is he a . . . Chicano?

Yeah, she said, like it was obvious. Of course he is. What did you think? And why would that question offend me?

It must be very hard for you and your family.

What?

To live with a Chicano.

Hello?

Being a Mexican girl and all, I thought that would bother you.

First of all, I'm not a girl. I'm a woman. Secondly, tengo sangre mexicana, pero I was born here. If you're trying to exoticize me, you better look for another señorita. This mujer is one hundred percent Chicana. Do you understand that? One hundred percent!

You're . . . Chicana?

Cien por ciento. She sat back in her chair, looked away, crossed her arms, like she was upset. After he paid the bill, she said, I'd like you to take me home now.

She stood up and walked out of the restaurant and waited for him on the sidewalk, her arms crossed.

She walked ahead of him, toward the car.

You didn't tell me you were Chicano, he said.

She stopped walking. She turned around, like she was ready to fight. What?!

I wouldn't have come to pick you up. I'm not interested in that. Believe me . . .

You racist bastard.

Me racist? Ha! I love Mexicans. I love Mexico. But Chicanos, I want nothing to do with them.

Fuck off, Stalin, she said, and she walked off. She passed a bunch of Chicano boys and started talking to them, and it looked to him like she was talking about him.

Misha looked down on his red T-shirt. It was bright red, impunity red, it was red. They were looking at him. He was wearing red. He was going to die for the color red. Then they started walking toward him.

He imagined he saw one of them putting his hands in his pants, as if going for a gun. He ran out of the boardwalk, down a side street and into an alley, and across a busy street. A few cars had to slam on their brakes, the drivers yelling out the windows. He ran and ran, just like a hero in the movies, or a video game avatar, running through alleys, pushing himself through bushes, jumping over sleeping dogs.

# THE ENCHANTED TIKI ROOM

He was fed up with the little brat and just wanted to be by himself for a while. He wanted to ask his wife would she mind if he took a walk alone, met up with them in a few hours, but he knew she would be hurt.

"How many times have you been here?" the little girl asked him.

"Like I told you, I used to work here," he said, "so it's impossible to say."

"You worked at Disneyland!?" said the girl, so excited. "It must have been the funnest job ever!"

"Like I said before, it was hard work," he said. "I had to go around the park with a broom and a dustpan, and I got hot and sweaty."

He was twenty-five back then, having just graduated with a degree in history from UCLA, and that was his last summer in California before heading to law school in Boston. He remembered that in order to work at Disneyland he had to cut his hair above the ears, a cut he didn't want, but afterward he thought it was a good, professional look, and he never had long hair after that.

Before he had worked at Disneyland, he came when he was nineteen years old, with a girlfriend whose name he forgot. She was a white girl, blonde hair, blue eyes, maybe Heather or Claire. He remembered how bored he was with the park, how everything seemed so corny and stupid, and all he wanted to do was to find a hotel, because on the drive over, Heather or Claire said that when they find a hotel they should take a shower together. He had never taken a shower with a woman, or spent the night with one in a hotel.

"You can wash my hair," she said.

Now, he was fifty-three, and he was walking into Adventure Land with his new family. Jenny was a kindergarten teacher he had met in a bar. They did shots all night, and after two weeks of texting each other, they had their first date.

Now, as they walked arm in arm, her little girl ran ahead too fast, into the entrance of Adventure Land, and Jenny yelled, "Get back here! Now!"

The girl slowly walked back to them, her head down, as if she had been slapped. They were passing by the Enchanted Tiki Room, something he'd forgot even existed.

He remembered now the first time he had come to Disneyland. He was about seven or eight. His mom wanted to see the Tiki Room.

She had read about it, she said, but the kids wanted to go on the rides, and the father was grumpy and kept complaining about the prices. When they walked through Adventure Land on the way to the haunted house, his mother just stopped. Everyone kept walking before they noticed she was missing, and they turned around and saw her standing before the entrance of the Enchanted Tiki Room.

"What are you doing?" asked his father, irritated with her.

"I'm going in," she said.

"You want to waste four tickets on a dumb show?" he asked, because back then, each attraction required a ticket.

"You can meet up later if you want," she said. "But I'm going to see it. I hear it's lovely." She went up the steps and inside the wide doors, and the family had no choice but to follow her.

He had forgotten all about this, and the other times he'd been in Disneyland he simply walked by the attraction, not even slightly interested in seeing it. It was one of the oldest attractions at the park, one of the first uses of animatronics. By now the technology must be dated.

He said to his new wife, who was from El Paso and had never been to Disneyland, "We should go see the Tiki Room."

"Is it a rollercoaster?" she asked. "You know I won't go on one."

"No, it's a show," he said. "You just sit and watch."

"Watch what?" asked the little girl, but he didn't remember. In his mind he saw lights and colors and maybe birds.

"Let's find out!"

"As long as it's not a rollercoaster," said his new wife.

"I love rollercoasters!" said the daughter. "I hope it's a rollercoaster!"

"It's not a rollercoaster," he said. "It's a show of some kind."

The boy at the entrance told them that the show would be starting in ten minutes, so they waited by the doors. The girl saw that they were selling pineapple ice cream and asked if she could have one. "You just had a churro," Jenny said. The girl pouted.

"My mom loved this," he said to Jenny. His mom had been dead for years.

"What did she like about it?" asked Jenny.

"I don't remember," he said.

He only remembered her face, how determined she was to see the show, how she ignored the snide comments of her husband, and that made her look strong and beautiful. The father said he would sit it out, and he walked across the path and entered an arcade.

When the doors opened and people were allowed inside, the girl said again, "I hope this is a rollercoaster!"

He looked around. The theater was an arena, seats on four sides, so his family was sitting opposite other families, like they were a mirror of themselves. He might have even looked at all the people sitting down to see if he could recognize his old family, try to imagine where they would have sat.

The lights went out, and the show started with a bird talking in a South American accent. He told some jokes and then some other birds came in and talked and they all started singing. The music was upbeat and tropical. He liked it.

Then birds with exotic feathers came down from the ceiling like Las Vegas showgirls and sang the chorus.

He watched his new wife, as if he was looking for something.

Her eyes were big and brown. He could tell she was enjoying the show, and that meant a lot to him.

He turned back to the birds, and that was when he saw across from them, on the other side of the singing birds, a little skinny boy who looked like him when he was that age. It made him smile even though he felt sad. The boy looked around the Enchanted Tiki Room as if everything was new and wonderful.

He knew all the bad things that would happen to the boy, addictions, love, and other natural disasters.

He turned to Jenny. "Do you see that boy?"

Red-and-blue birds were sparkling in her eyes. He could see them moving their wings, opening and closing their mouths as they sang, tapping their talons to the beat of the drums. He watched the show in the windows of her eyes and imagined he could walk into them.

He looked around to see if he could spot the boy's parents, wanting to see his family, but no one looked familiar.

His stepdaughter pulled his arm and whispered in his ear. "Can we go on a rollercoaster next?"

He looked in her eyes, so fat with want, and he said, "Sure." That one word made her happy.

He looked for the boy, but his seat was empty, and then he saw him leaving through a side door. He told Jenny that he had to go to the bathroom, and he got up.

In the hallway, he saw the boy go into the men's room, so the man followed.

When he entered, the boy was using the urinal, and when he was done, he washed his little hands, looking at himself and making faces in the mirror. The man was in the corner of the reflection, but the boy didn't seem to notice, and he left.

The man pretended to wash his hands, and then he followed the boy outside.

He looked just like the pictures his father took of their day at Disneyland. In fact, he remembered more about the pictures they took than the day itself. He had a haircut the shape of a bowl, chubby cheeks, and he wore Mickey Mouse ears and held onto his mother while his sister was on the other side of her. Goofy was standing behind them, tall and smiling, waving at the camera.

"Mister?"

The boy was looking up at him. He looked seven years old.

"What is it?" he asked.

"How do you get to the birds?"

"Come on," he said, "follow me," and he led the kid toward the entrance. "What's your name?" he asked.

"Billy."

"I'm William."

"That's really my name, too," said the boy. "But my mom only calls me that when she's mad."

They walked into the Enchanted Tiki Room, but it was empty and dark, and the birds were mute and unmoving.

"Where is everybody?" Billy asked.

"Not sure," said the man. "I guess the show's over."

He patted his pocket for his phone so he could text Jenny, but it wasn't there. "Come on," he said. They walked out the doors but there was no one around.

"Where's my mom?" said the boy.

The man took the boy's hand and led him out of the waiting area into the stream of people, hundreds of them walking by, kids with Mickey ears, young mothers pushing strollers, teenagers running to the next ride, but they somehow looked strange, as if the saturation were toned down and the film was grainy.

Then he approached a Disney employee, a young woman standing at the entrance of a souvenir shop. She had a nametag and wore a flouncy dress like from a western saloon.

"Excuse me," he said. "I have a lost kid here. Can you help us find his parents?" She just stood there smiling at the people passing.

"Excuse me!" he said louder, but she didn't see him.

"How come she don't say nothing?" said the boy.

"*Doesn't* say *anything*," said the man. "I don't know."

"Maybe we're in the mirror," said the boy.

"What do you mean?"

"Maybe in the bathroom we passed through the mirror. Like Alice."

"I forgot about that," he said, remembering how after learning of Alice's adventures, the boy could look into a mirror for hours, imagining a parallel universe, imagining another version of himself.

"Excuse me," he said to the stream of people passing by, but no one stopped, no one saw them, as if they were invisible.

"Hey!" he yelled, but nothing. The faces streamed by like an 8-mm film. "Can anyone hear me??"

"We are here! We are here! We are here!" the boy yelled, Horton-like.

"Let's go find a police officer," William said, and as they walked through the crowd, Billy held his hand tightly.

Then he saw something he knew was going to make the day weirder.

A young man and a pretty young woman were waiting in line at a popcorn vendor.

The woman was dressed like it was the 1980s, a lot of curled blonde hair cascading from her head, and she wore tight, shiny pants and a bright orange tank top. The young man had shoulder-length hair, feathered back, and he wore a Member's Only jacket.

"That's my jacket," said William, and he knew he was looking at himself at nineteen. The girl was the one he'd come with, but he couldn't remember her name.

He walked over to them, and when the young man saw both versions of himself, he dropped his popcorn, which flew all over like magic dust.

"Do I know you?" he said to the man and the boy.

"He's looking for his mother," the man said.

"This is weird," said the teenager.

All three of them stood looking at each other, a triangle of confusion. "What's your name?" asked the man.

"Billy," said the teenager.

"That's my name!" said the boy.

"What's your girlfriend's name? I forgot."

"You forgot *Melissa*? How's that possible?"

"Melissa," the man repeated, imagining himself looking through his memory files for some sort of a-ha! moment, but the name didn't sound familiar.

He remembered the magic that would happen in the hotel that night, a fond memory he would carry for years, but not much else about her, not even how or why they broke up. Now Melissa was eating popcorn, but she was on the other side of whatever separated them from the others, and her colors were muted and she acted as if she didn't know they were there.

The teenager told Melissa to wait right there for him, he would be right back, and the three of them walked into the crowds.

"What do you do for a living?" asked the teenager.

"I'm not an actor," he said. "Sorry."

"Then what?" he asked, clearly disappointed.

"University administrator. A dean."

"What's a dean?" asked the little boy.

"Someone boring," said the teenager.

"Let's go down Main Street," said the man. "They have a City Hall where they answer questions, and we can find Security there. Maybe we can find out what's going on."

"What happens to Melissa?" asked the teen.

"Hey look!" said the boy, and they all saw a Disney employee sweeping the floor and gathering debris in a dustpan. The employee was brighter than everyone else in their view, as if heat was coming from his body. As he swept he was humming a song they all knew.

*Catch a falling star and put it in your pocket never let it fade away.*

"Excuse me," William said, and the employee turned around. His nametag said Bill.

He was twenty-five and clean-cut, working there for the summer before he had to leave for Boston and law school.

When he saw them, he dropped his broom.

"What was I thinking?" he said, looking at the teenager's feathered, shoulder-length hair and 1980s clothes.

"Hey, this is cutting edge," said the teen.

"You look like a clown."

"That's enough," said William. "We have to find out what's going on."

Now there were four of them walking down Main Street, the people flowing by them like a stream of ghosts.

"Maybe we all got out of the mirror," said the little boy.

"What mirror?" asked Bill the Disney employee.

"In the Enchanted Tiki Room," said the boy.

At the words "Enchanted Tiki Room" all of them stopped and looked around, but none of them was looking for the same thing.

The man looked for other versions of himself, the teenager looked for Melissa, and the employee was looking for a clock so he would know the time, because he still had to sweep up around the Matterhorn. He held on to the broom and dustpan. The boy was looking at a magic shop.

"Come on," said William. "Let's not just stand around here. Let's go to City Hall."

"So, am I a lawyer?" asked Bill.

"We changed our mind. Law didn't suit us."

"What did?"

"He's a dean," said the teen.

"Where?" Bill asked him.

"University of Texas, El Paso."

"That's not what we wanted," said the twenty-five-year-old. "I thought we would live in New York."

William shrugged.

"Do I ever get married?" asked the nineteen-year-old. He touched his hair to make sure it was all in place. "Do I ever get to date that perfume girl at Macy's? Will I ever know her name?"

"Look!! Look!!" screamed the boy. "Can we go in?! Please! Please! Can we go in??"

The taller ones looked at the boy and then followed his finger to where it was presumably pointing, Houdini's Magic Shop.

"Please!?"

"Not now. We need to find out what's going on. Ask your mom to take you later."

But three of them knew his mom wouldn't take him later, that his mom and dad would end up in a big fight, and on their way out of the park, when they passed the Magic Shop, he begged them to go inside but she ignored him. His father raised his hand and told him to shut up.

The older man remembered something else, but only by watching the teenager looking at the Magic Shop. He remembered that he and the girl called Melissa were walking around the park and something about the Magic Shop gripped him. He wanted to go in and take a look. He now remembered entering the store, as if walking into a magician's lair. He had been so bored with Disney that day, only wanting to get to the hotel, wanting to wash Melissa's hair, but now he was excited about the magic.

The young man who worked the counter back in the 1980s was funny and charismatic. He was tall and thin and wore a straw hat like from a barbershop quartet. His nametag said Steve. There was a crowd of people watching as he told jokes and did magic tricks to their oohs! and aahs!

The teenager, who wanted to be an actor back then, thought Steve had the best job in the world, and he vowed someday he too would work at Disneyland. He would be an actor.

Steve showed the crowd three red balls in his hand, and he waved one hand over the other, closed his fist and opened it, and the balls had disappeared.

"That's pretty cool," the teenager said to Melissa.

He ended up buying those little red balls and trying to learn it the way Steve had shown them. They were made of spongy material that you could squeeze into tiny dots and tuck under your fingers, which made them seem like they disappeared.

For the rest of the day he was eager to get back to the hotel to try them out. That's all he did in the hotel that night, practice magic, trying to get it right, long after Melissa had fallen asleep. And he got it right! He had a knack for magic. He was doing magic!

"Can we go in?" pleaded the little boy.

"Let's just go in," said the nineteen-year-old, and they all agreed.

They walked in, saw walls lined with color and magic tricks. Behind the counter was a very old man, and at first the teenager wondered if it was Steve, who had been so funny and talented. The old man was looking down on a ledger, writing numbers in it with a red pen, and when he looked up at the four, they saw his nametag. Dr. Chavez.

"How old are you?" asked Bill.

"Eighty-five," said the old man.

"I guess that's a good sign."

"But look at those wrinkles!" said the teenager.

"We earned them," said the old man.

The little boy looked around at everyone.

"Are we family?" he asked.

"We are," said the old man. "And you, my friend, are your own angel. All of you are."

"He becomes a dean!" said Bill, embittered. "We were going to be a lawyer!"

"You mean an actor," said the teenager. "It's all we ever wanted."

The old man looked at the teenager and sighed. "I would probably not even recognize you if it wasn't for the images I scanned and uploaded into The Wall'."

"The what?"

"Do you want to know what I do?" said the old man. "I work here ten hours a week. But just for fun. I'm retired. I discovered, or I should say I rediscovered, that I like magic."

"Is Jenny with you?" asked William.

"Come on," said the old man. "I want to show you something all of you forgot."

"Is she with you?" he asked again. "What happens to Jenny?"

"What happens to Melissa?" asked the teen.

"Follow me."

The old man led them out onto the plaza before the Main Street entrance. The balloons of a vendor passed by them like colorful clouds.

"This way," said the old man. He led them down Main Street to a café on the corner. "You forgot this," he said. "Don't forget again."

He walked into the area with tables, all of them full, and they followed.

Sitting at a table was a young mother and a little boy, himself at seven years old. His mom was so young, maybe still in her twenties.

The boy saw his mother, and he ran over there yelling, "Mama!" and his body wisped into a ghost and he entered the boy.

They remembered it now. It happened right after they had left the Enchanted Tiki Room. His father and his sister were getting the food while he and his mom sat at a table. She was silent.

She looked off in the distance, as if imagining herself in a better place. "It was so beautiful," she said.

"What was?" the boy asked.

"The Tiki Room. So amazing."

"It was just a bunch of stupid birds," he said.

"No, no," said the mother. "It was more than that." She looked right at the boy. "They looked so real, didn't they? But they were animatronics!"

"What's that mean?"

"They were man-made!"

"You mean they were fake? But everyone knows that!"

The mother heard a bird and looked up into the trees.

"Things are going to change," she said. "Don't you see? They're going to get better."

The father and sister came back with the food. He was grouchy. "You better eat every bite," he said. "This cost a week's worth of groceries!"

Everyone dug into their burgers and fries, except his mother, who continued to look into the trees and the birds flitting and singing. She leaned into the boy and said only to him, "Think of the possibilities. They create living things, real personalities, from parts of metal and wire and rubber." She tapped her nails on the table. "Think of the possibilities."

Of course, he didn't understand.

"Someday, maybe we can put our own spirits into machines. Or robots. Or computers! Someplace where they can store our consciousness! Everything we've ever felt and thought about. Who knows where we'll be floating around inside of the ether! Imagine the possibilities!"

"Just shut up and eat," said the father.

"Anything's possible," she whispered to the boy, looking into his eyes. "Do you believe?"

"Yes," he said. "I believe."

# PART TWO

# THE CAULDRON

Let me have the paella mixta, an order of fries, patatas bravas, a plate of cheese and sausage . . . and a bottle of the Rioja.

The waiter put down his pad and said, Are you sure? That paella is meant to feed four people. It's a lot of food.

My friends will be joining me, said the man.

The waiter looked at the two empty seats, lifted his pad, and continued to write the order. Then he left for the kitchen.

He pushed the door and it opened and swung back and forth, and he walked into the heat. The cooks were throwing steaks onto the fire, the flames hissing and rising. Before he picked up an armful of plates for table ten, he pulled the phone from his pocket and looked at the screen. No texts.

He brought out the wine first, uncorked it, placed three glasses, two in the empty spots across from the man and one in front of the man.

I guess you'll do the tasting, said the waiter, trying to be funny.

No need, said the man, just pour.

So he did, a glass for the man, and then he put the bottle on the table and was about to leave when the man said, Can you pour the other two, please?

The waiter looked at the empty glasses, the empty chairs. For your friends?

Yes, said the man, for my friends.

The waiter poured. The wine took its time, the velvety red swirling around the glass like a liquid tail.

When he delivered the bread, he put down three small plates, one in front of the man and the other two in the empty spots across from him. He noticed the man had barely touched the wine, but the other two glasses were a different case. One of them was empty and the other was about a quarter full. But the chairs were still empty and there was no sign of the man's dinner companions.

Are your friends late? he asked.

In a manner of speaking.

The waiter took a pair of tongs and put a slice of bread on the man's plate. He was about to go, but the man cleared his throat and that stopped the waiter. The man looked at the empty plates.

You want me to serve them now? said the waiter, and the man nodded.

The waiter put a piece of bread on each plate, feeling like he was being watched.

Then he went to check up on table ten, across the room, make sure they had everything they wanted. There were nine people on ten.

The cheese and sausage came next, and the waiter noticed that the bread he had served on the other two plates had been eaten. On one plate, half the slice was bitten off, and on the other, there were only a few crumbs. The bread on the man's plate was still whole.

Is everything okay? said the waiter, and he looked at the man's plate, and the man looked at his plate and said, I don't have much of an appetite.

The waiter looked at the other two plates.

Are they still . . . coming? You're friends?

No, Pablo, there are already here.

The waiter felt shivers down his back, and at first he thought it was because the man somehow knew his name, Pablo, but then he remembered he was wearing a nametag, so he wasn't sure why he was so freaked out.

Can you pour more wine? the man asked.

The only wineglasses that needed more were standing behind the empty places, but the waiter shrugged and poured anyway.

On his way back to the kitchen, the waiter figured the guy was just lonely, and so he had to make up friends. There were a lot of weird people in the city. One time a lady came in with three white dogs, wanting all of them to sit at the table with her.

He looked at the man sitting alone, and he shrugged again and walked to the bar to get more drinks for table ten. They were getting loud.

By the time the potatoes were delivered, the cheese and the meat were gone from the empty places.

They loved it, said the man. Thank you.

The cheese was still on the man's plate. You didn't?

I don't have much of an appetite, he said again, as if ashamed.

That's okay, said the waiter actually feeling sorry for the man, but then he remembered that it was bullshit, the man was eating everything and he had some sort of guilt complex for being so gluttonous. The man was crazy.

He wasn't fat.

If this was his way of eating to excess without feeling guilty, he must not have always done it, not every day.

The man was tall and thin and had an angular face with a protruding chin. He looked a bit like those old actors in black-and-white movies, like Kirk Douglas. He kind of looked like an angel.

But he was just a crazy man.

The waiter went toward the kitchen, but for some reason he wanted to see the man eat off the empty plates, just to prove to himself how crazy the man was/is. So he hid inside the busboy station, where he could see the man through the crack between two slats. The man was talking to the invisible others as if they were there, and he even paused to listen to what the other two were saying. A busboy passed in front of the waiter and started to unload dishes onto a tray. If he wanted to see the man eat, he'd have to find his way back to the floor. He went out there to pretend to be checking on a table, but by the time he was able to see the man, the two plates in front of the empty seats were wiped clean. He walked over there.

Your paella should be ready soon, he told the man.

Thank you, said the man, looking at his own wrist, maybe where a watch used to be. The nails on his long fingers looked manicured.

The waiter delivered the paella, looked at the empty seats, looked at the man, and served the first plate.

The man waited for him to serve the other two.

I don't understand, said the waiter.

Pablo, said the man. We want you to know that you're doing a great job. Especially considering what's going on in your life. It can't be easy.

But how . . . ?

The man looked over where the other two people would be, and then slowly he looked back at the waiter.

We want you to know that it'll be okay, said the man. We promise. Everything will be fine.

I've never been so scared in my life, the waiter said, trying his best not to break down.

Trust us. Things will be okay. Okay?

The waiter wanted to believe them, or, er . . . him.

He nodded, and then he jerked up and wanted to get back to being a professional.

Can I get you anything else? he asked.

The man looked at one of the empty places as if he were listening to someone sitting there. He nodded, then he turned to the waiter.

Another bottle of the Rioja.

# THE *AND NE FORHTEDON NÁ!*

The bookseller held them up to show to me, one volume in each hand, but he kept coughing on them, the wet spray from his mouth landing on the hardback covers.

I wanted them badly.

I would have paid a lot, but I had to be realistic and ask myself, Was I willing to die for them?

"Very old books," he said, catching his breath. "Antiques."

They were in perfect condition if not for the saliva dripping off them, and yes, maybe I'm exaggerating. Maybe I didn't actually see them wet with his germs, but I knew they were there, because germs were everywhere, and this tubercular bookseller looked like he was about to die, his face skeletal, his eyes red and watery, and he even had blue lips like a zombie. He couldn't stop hacking phlegm onto his bicep.

"I don't read," he said. "So I can't tell you if it's a good story, but," he said, with a *hack hack hack* into his sleeve. "But they'll look real good in your home. You can put them on a shelf and people will see them."

He didn't know what they were, but I did, and I wanted them.

These two books were a collection of apocryphal gospels compiled and edited by Jorge Luis Borges, questionable passages from Luke, Matthew, Mark, and John, and some from a fifth gospel.

I knew that dark bodies of old men in robes and jewels sat around tables, each of them with a shadowy herald standing behind him, and like editors of a literary magazine, they rejected most of the stories to be included in the Bible. They probably refused to read some after the first page. And here they were gathered, all the rejects Borges had chosen.

As a writer with nine unsold novels and a stack of rejected stories, I wanted to see why these gospels in particular didn't grab the attention of those decrepit old men in robes.

I wanted to know why God's editors rejected these stories, but they had a film of moisture from the bookseller's mouth.

We were in the zócalo on a Sunday, and across the plaza was the cathedral, looming large over the market like Kafka's castle, and suddenly the bells began to ring the tune that signaled they were about to bong the hours.

I decided I would play a game.

I decided that by the end of the bongs I would have decided whether or not to buy the books.

"You want to hold them?" the bookseller asked. I would have to consider the pros and cons.

*Bong!*

I could die.

*Bong!*

But I could have the bookseller put them in a plastic bag, and I'd wipe them with disinfectant when I get home. I could start reading them right away, and I might like the form and start writing my own apocryphal gospels. I needed to write something that would justify me, my life, and to paraphrase Baudelaire, to show my enemies how superior I am to them. I don't mean that seriously, but rather as a reminder that if I cannot make any money this year off writing, I have to find a job. The money from the lawsuit was running out, and I knew my brothers and sister wouldn't share theirs.

*Bong!*

They could be fun to read. Fun is desire in progress.

*Bong!*

Fuck it. I bring the books home, take them out of the bag, and start licking them, I mean, slopping them up like a juicy mango, and I swallow the taste of the bookseller's saliva and catch whatever nasty disease he has.

*Bong!*

That dark body of judges decreed that this bookseller in this plaza on this Sunday in this city, El Distrito Federál, is *not* inspired by the Holy Spirit, so he must die. He must choke on his own bile, but first, he must contaminate all the books he has, so that anyone who dares to read them dares death.

*Bong!*

*Jesus said to the multitudes, There was a certain bookseller who was dying of consumption and he didn't even know how to read.*
*Imagine that! All your life surrounded by piles of books, un montón de texts, but not being able to read a single one.*

*Bong!*

What the fuck! Buy the books.

*Bong!*

*And ne forhtedon ná!*
On Borges's grave, which I visited in Geneva when I was a young man, I saw written on his stone, *And ne forhtedon ná!*, and it took me years to find out what it meant (this was before Google). It was Old English for "Be not afraid," and I thought of facing death bravely, saying over and over to myself, *And ne forhtedon ná!* And throughout the years, that phrase, the *And ne forhtedon ná!*, became words I'd say to myself before I entered a room or opened a door or walked alone into a crowded café. It became my sign of the cross.

*Bong!*

*I am a sick man! I am a spiteful man!*
　　I am a happy man! I am a generous man!
　　*Girls just want to have fu-un!*

　*Bong!*

"Those who restrain desire do so because theirs is weak enough to be restrained."

　　I am ruled by desire.

　　I want those books.

　　Desire is energy, and I must channel it into action. I will have those books.

　　On the other hand, don't the Kabbalists say that the gift of desire is desire itself, not the attainment of what is desired? Maybe my *desire* for the books is what matters most.

　*Bong!*

"How much do you want for them?" I asked.

　　He named a price one hundred times lower than what I had expected, the cost of a hotdog from a street vendor. I handed him the exact amount and asked him to put them in a sack.

　　*Jesus came from the desert, and he came upon a bookseller.*

　　*"Bless my tomes," pleaded the man. "I am with consumption and will die soon. I want to make sure my wife and children are well fed and that there will always be ducks in our pond."*

　　*Jesus said, "I will do more than put ducks in your pond. I will heal you."*

　　*"That sounds awesome! What do I have to do to receive this gift?"*

　　*"Read this pamphlet. It will tell all you need to be saved."*

　　*"I don't read."*

　　*"Too bad, so sad!" Jesus cried.*

# KAFKA IN A SKIRT

1.

I want to eat breakfast with you.

I'm sure you would.

No, I'm sorry. I don't mean *that*. I mean I'd like to pick you up and take you out to breakfast.

That's odd. I've never been asked out to breakfast. Unless it's a business thing.

Well, I want to go out with you. I have for a while now, which I'm sure was obvious to you.

Yup. The way you look at me sometimes is kind of, I don't know, ambiguous.

So, I want to go out with you, and I know this . . . really nice place, a breakfast place.

She put down the stack of papers she had been carrying across the office when he had asked her did she have a minute. She had been holding them for a long time and her arms were tired. Arms free, she faced him, hands on her hips, with confidence. They were in the copy room of Black Kitten Publishers.

On the wall was a glossy poster with a businesswoman carrying a huge computer monitor as she runs across a field, one of those old fat computers that used floppy disks. Her hair is disheveled, and she's running toward a giant metal wall so tall you can't see the other side.

The wall expands across the curve of the land and the top of it touches the clouds, where light streams out and shines on her face. The caption on the poster reads, YOUR DATA IS SAFE IN THE WALL®.

I guess breakfast makes sense for a first date, she said. This is a date you're asking me on?

Absolutely! Let me make that perfectly clear.

It's a safe date, she thought. Breakfast. Okay, she said, and then, in the voice of Eddie Murphy's Donkey, she exclaimed, Let's have some waffles!

I'll pick you up at seven, but I have to warn you. This is, uh, a somewhat formal place, so, you know, I'm going to wear a suit.

Are you saying I should wear . . .

An evening gown. If you want to. I mean, I'm going to be pretty dressed up.

An evening gown for breakfast?

This is a special place.

Well, now I'm curious.

Oh, and it could last several hours. Just so you know.

What kind of breakfast is this?

He put his hands in his pockets and pushed his fists down and said, A really good breakfast.

## 2.

She walked down the front steps in an evening gown, carrying a tiny purse, and he waited on the bottom of the steps looking up, watching her. His shadow waited next to him on the sidewalk, like a buddy.

When she reached him, he reached for her elbow and led her to his car, but his shadow went in the opposite direction. She wore diamond earrings that she hadn't worn since her divorce, so she kept touching them.

He opened the door for her but didn't wait for her to get inside.

The car was tiny and old and smelled of gas. She had expected he would drive an expensive car, all blinking lights and talking computers, but this was a piece of junk, and she thought she might like him more because of that.

Still, she thought, looking around the car, he could be neater.

In one corner on the backseat there was an open box, inside of which were books, the same book by the same author, multiple copies, *A Fist on the Moon* by Nora Muñoz.

She reached into the backseat and grabbed *the Moon.*

She saw a circle of trees in a meadow and a full moon shining down. Three girls in white dresses stood in the circle, in a triangle facing each other, and they were all looking up at the moon, which shone on their dresses, white, white, Wicca-like.

She liked the image.

She looked at the back, but there was no author's picture.

She opened it and read the name of the publishing house, which she had never heard of, 3 Sisters Press. She turned the page and read the epigraph.

> *¡Señor Alcade, sus hijas están mirando a la luna!*
>
> LORCA

As a third-generation Latina, her Spanish wasn't that good, but the quote was obviously referring to "daughters" and the "moon" and maybe a mayor of a small town.

She turned the book over and looked at the blurbs on the back cover, first at the names, to see if she recognized any of the writers. She didn't, so she read the first blurb.

*This book makes you wonder.*

Is this a good book? she wondered aloud.

Well . . . to be honest. It's okay.

Why do you have so many copies?

I knew the girl.

Girl?

Well, the woman. The writer. She's dead.

## 3.

He told her, These are my author's copies.

I don't understand.

Nora died before her book came out, he said, and I own the rights. They sent me twenty copies, and I was going to promote it, I mean really get the word out, but I guess I never got around to it. Time, you know.

She opened the book and looked at the copyright date.

That box has been back there for a few years now, he said. Take one. I can't get you a signed copy for obvious reasons, but you can have one if you want. Take two! Give one to a friend. But, look, I'll be honest . . . Nora was my . . . uh, a "friend," I guess you could say. She was always writing. I would ask her to stop, to come out for a drink, meet some people, take a walk, but she was always locked in her room writing stories. Well, about a week before she died, she invited me into her writing room, which she had never done before. Everything was white. The desk. The chairs. The bookshelves. The walls. The few paintings on the walls were mostly white too, with a dash of bright red or blue. She had all the windows open, and the sun made everything even more white and warm. She had a black-and-white photo on the wall behind her desk, an Argentinian poet she liked. I forget her name, but she was Jewish and young, and she killed herself.

So Nora sat at her desk, and I sat opposite her. She was wearing a white skirt that day. It was really short.

Excuse me? Why is that an important detail? That her skirt was *really short*?

He shrugged and continued. Nora told me she wanted me to take possession of all her writings. Everything she's ever written, ever. In the event of her death, which—when I think about it now is kind of creepy—she wanted me to destroy it all. Every word. I expected she would hand me boxes and boxes of her work, but all she handed me was a napkin folded in two.

A napkin?

Yeah, so I unfold it and it says, Alejandra#^5*.

Her password for The Wall'. She had always written on computers and smartphones and iPads. She had no paper at all.

Delete everything, she said. Of course, of course, I said, but I looked around her office and thought maybe Nora was a genius, like Kafka. I was like Max Broad. Aren't we better off that Max *didn't* obey his dying friend's wish? So after Nora died, I went into The Wall' and found, among other things, a completed collection of stories. She called it *Your Daughters Are Looking at the Moon.*

I sent it to a publisher, just to see what they thought about it.

Then I went through all the other documents she had, thousands of them. After reading and reading, I realized she wasn't that good. I ended up deleting everything, just like she had asked me to. Then a few months later I heard from the publisher that they wanted to publish her book.

He looked at *the Moon* in her hands.

Why is it called *A Fist on the Moon*? she asked.

I changed the title, he said. I liked it better than hers.

Oh, no! she said, looking at the book. It's a warning to men. Beware when your daughters look at the moon!

He cleared his throat. Well, he said. The book isn't great. The stories are redolent of workshop fiction. There seem to be too many epiphanies, as if there was no *going*, only arriving.

## 4.

She didn't want that to be true. She wanted Muñoz to be a genius, thinking that he was just being arrogant, thinking he could mansplain a book written by a strong woman. He probably didn't even understand it.

They were on a desert road going east, the orange of the rising sun washing the dashboard and their faces with morning light.

She thumbed through the book. The white pages glowed orange. How did she die? she asked.

Her body shut down. I don't know. They explained it to me.

She stopped on a story called "Boy in the Basement."

It was about a woman named Emily who liked to sit by the window and read stories. One Saturday, settling down in her velvet armchair, she read about a Mexican boy who lived in the basement of a retired couple. They didn't charge him rent because the Mexican boy kept the yard clean. He was a nice boy.

But one day the old man was pulling his Crown Victoria into the driveway when he saw a spark in the basement window.

Maybe the flick of a lighter to a glass pipe? He knew about meth, and this boy was from Juárez and barely spoke English.

The man went to the window and looked inside.

Tchaikovsky was playing, and the boy danced like a ballerina, twirling with such grace and lightness, twirling like a petal in the wind, rising off the ground and landing on his toe and twirling on it.

He had never seen anything so beautiful in his life, but then a shadow came up behind the boy . . .

We're here! he said, pulling the car into a dirt lot next to an old white house. Get ready for a great breakfast.

<h1 style="text-align:center">5.</h1>

The white house had three stories, multiple windows with white curtains.

He led her by the elbow across the lawn to the house. There were some people hanging around outside on the porch.

Who are they? she asked.

These are people who didn't make reservations, he said. They may not make it inside, but they'll wait, just for the possibility. But don't worry. I made reservations way in advance.

There was an old blind man sitting on a wicker chair, leaning forward on his white cane. Sitting on a porch swing were two middle-aged blonde women, dressed elegantly, and they were talking in Spanish about an artist. ¡Tal blanco! one said. ¡Blanco terrible! said the other.

There were two young men, business suits, their eyes red and ties undone.

A man, by himself, paced across the lawn, looking worried. He wore a long, black coat, past his knees, made of fine and shiny material. Under his coat he wore a silk suit tailored for his slim body. A gold watch shone on his wrist. He kept looking at it and shaking his head in disbelief.

*Way* in advance? it occurred to her. You just asked me yesterday.

I guess I hoped you would say yes.

She wasn't sure how she felt about that.

They got to the front door.

He opened it, and the light shone on her face.

She covered her eyes.

Come in! he said. Come in!

# WATER AND DOG

The father said, Go ahead, Son. Pick one.

Really?

Yeah, do it. Thirteen is important.

The boy looked at the shiny bottles on the shelf, and he wanted a big one, something that he could share, but he didn't want his father to spend too much, because his father was always complaining about deductions, so he grabbed the small bottle, 170 milliliters.

Are you sure that's the one you want?

Yes, please.

The father took the bottle and walked up to the cash-bot.

He put his thumb on the pad.

His son was right behind him, looking at the bottle, practically licking his lips.

When I was a kid, he told his son as he watched the cash-bot calculate the deduction, hoping there was enough, there used to be water fountains everywhere, cold, delicious water, everywhere, and free.

Oh, come on, Dad. I'm thirteen.

No, I'm serious. They were everywhere. Public parks, stores, they even had them in the schools. Sometimes there were three or four spigots in the same fountain, and all you had to do was twist the lever and four kids could drink at the same time, as much water as you wanted.

I don't believe that, said the boy.

We didn't need hydro-pills back then. Or semiannual injections.

Thank you for shopping at eMart, said the cash-bot, spitting out the data.

All true, said the father, handing the bottle of water to his boy.

That's rather hard to believe, he said, holding up the bottle, his eyes wide, to look at it. It would be his first time with his own water.

Are you going to drink it now?

Not now. I want to save some. I want this to last.

They left the eMart and walked into the tunnel-walk.

So, if water was free, the boy asked, how come they didn't tell us that in history class?

False history, the father said.

I don't get it, said the boy.

That's all you get, said the man. They only tell us what they think we should know.

There was a commotion in the plaza. A crowd of people.

The boy ran up ahead to see what it was.

The father, left behind, looked at his thumb and sighed. Thirteen is an important number, he said to himself.

The boy ran back, excited. Dad! A dog! A real dog!

Really? asked the father, and they ran to the plaza, breaking through the crowd, the father holding his son's hand, taking him to the front.

Sure enough, on a wagon pulled by twin ladies in red tights and blonde wigs was a dog, a small one with big ears, sitting on a velvet pillow. He had his mouth open and his tongue slightly out.

The crowd surrounded the dog, but the ladies kept pulling the wagon and the people broke apart to let them through.

He's so cute! said the boy.

The dog was looking around at all the people, happy, and if he set his eyes on someone, the person winked twice to snap a neuro-pic and then posted it immediately onto The Wall'.

So cute! said the boy. He winked twice, two times. This is the best birthday ever! he thought, and it appeared as text with the pic and he sent it to his friends and family. He looked up at his dad, who looked a little sad. Are you okay, Dad?

When I was a boy, dogs were everywhere. There were so many swarming the earth that they had to put them in a kind of dog prison, "the pound," they called it. And if no one wanted them, and no one ever did, they gassed them.

Ok, Dad, said the boy. Whatever you say.

The dad started to cry, his shoulders moving up and down. He held down his head to hide the tears.

What's wrong, Dad? Are you okay?

I miss Droopy.

Here, Dad, take a drink. Please take a drink. The boy handed his father the bottle.

No, that's yours. He stood up in a gesture that said he was regaining his strength. He took a hydro-pill from his pocket and placed it on his tongue. Come on, he said. Let's do this. This is thirteen. Thirteen! Thirteen!

# YOU CAN'T DO THAT WITH A GOAT!

My brothers and sisters told me that she was the only tenant left, and that she not only had a right to stay there until she died, but that she was also grandfathered into the right to receive orders from our parrilla across the street. She was some relation to the old owner, and he made our father promise that no matter what happens, no matter what changes he might make to the restaurant, that she would still get her deliveries, even though there was no elevator in her building.

"She's really something," my youngest sister said as they prepared her order. "What do you mean?" I asked, and all my siblings laughed.

I was the youngest brother, having just started working with the family, so I had to be the one to climb all those stairs. They said she lived on the top floor, number 1302. They told me that she ordered the same thing every time, two humida empanadas, a caprese salad, and a bottle of Malbec. They said she was at least a hundred years old, about the age of the building, and she had never lived anywhere else in her life.

I took the order and crossed the street and entered the code to get into the building. The lobby was dark and quiet and I could hear myself breathe and walk.

I reached the winding staircase and looked up into the vortex, all the way to a square of light on the top floor, the only occupied apartment in the building.

I knew it was stupid, but I felt deep in my gut that when I got there, she would be dead. I started up the stairs, and they twisted up and around and around.

On each of the floors the lights were out, and I could barely see the numbers on the doors, just shadows of the numbers, like random shapes of some secret language.

When I finally arrived on the top floor, I couldn't see the number, but I knew which door had to be hers because it had a welcome mat, and on the door itself there was a picture some kid had drawn of a green field with a horse bending down eating grass, or maybe it was a cow.

I lifted the horse/cow drawing aside and saw the door number underneath, 1302, so I rang.

I heard it ring inside, and a few seconds later I was happy to hear her coming to the door. She was talking to someone.

"I can't believe they even had one!"

Her voice was husky but at the same time feminine, like an actress from the 1930s, one of those femme fatales who always smoked thin cigarettes in long cigarette holders.

"Are you joking with me?" she said. "They had one of *those*!?"

She opened the door, and I was surprised how young she was, and pretty. She wore a housedress, not quite a nightie, but like a silky housedress, bright red. It was kind of thin and short, but it wasn't tight or sexy or anything.

This will *not* turn out to be one of those pizza-delivery-boy porn stories. I'm gay and have no interest in heterosexual fantasies.

When I say she was pretty, I don't mean it the way most people mean pretty. In my memory, her face was Picasso pretty, because when I recall it, I see three equal parts: the eyes and bridge of the nose, the nose and mouth, and the forehead and eyes. Everything was set in its right place, but the pieces somehow didn't all fit together. Since I was the last one to see her alive, I was questioned by the police, but of course I didn't tell them she looked like a Picasso, because I would sound like a crazy man and they might think that I murdered her.

I remember one of her eyes had a red dot in it, so it was kind of off-putting to look at her.

She hardly looked at me standing in her doorway, as if I had been the one delivering to her for years.

She motioned for me to come in. She had on a wireless headset, and she was talking into it. "Come on, Flavio! Don't tell me you don't regret not going with them."

She listened to Flavio for a while, and I could hear his voice, quick and excited and a bit feminine, but I couldn't make out his words.

She laughed. "Me too! Me too! I've never even been close enough to see it!"

I could hear his voice getting more and more excited.

She laughed hard as she was pulling money out of her wallet. She gestured where I should put the food and wine, and then she handed me the cash.

I don't remember what her apartment looked like, that is, how it was decorated, what kind of furniture it had (for some reason Second Empire style comes to me, although I'm not even sure what that means). I remember how soft everything looked, chairs, coffee tables, doilies.

She had the blinds down and the curtains drawn, and the only light came from dim lamps.

I put down the food and fumbled in my pouch for her change, but she waved it off, indicating I should keep it.

I just stood there, as if waiting for something.

That was when I saw her ankles. They were thin, too thin, and I wondered how she could stand on them for long. Her legs were normal, but her ankles seemed so bony. And I noticed on one of the ankles, right above the bone that stuck out, was an open sore. It was red and purple, like it was flesh exposed to the air, and I imagined I could smell putrid meat.

I know the smell was only my imagination, but that's how I remember it, like dead animal, and as she stood there opening the bottle of wine and talking to Flavio, I couldn't stop looking at the sore.

She pulled out the cork, listening to Flavio tell his story. Then she screamed, "What??"

"You can't do *that* with a goat!" she yelled. She laughed and laughed and laughed.

What *couldn't* you do with a goat? I wondered.

I stood there, as if waiting for the answer.

She turned around and saw I was still there, and she looked irritated, so I thanked her and left.

As I descended the circling stairs I could hear her laugh, "You can't do *that* with a goat!"

# A STUPID COW

She stepped into the elevator. She watched him slide the cage-like outer door closed, then the inner doors slid closed on their own. The red plastic card he held said 1216. He pressed the button for the twelfth floor.

In my country, he said, in her language, there's no such thing as floor zero.

No? she asked. How could that be?

Over there floor zero is called the first floor, so the first floor here, for us, is the second floor for you guys.

He looked at the card in his hand, 1216. Back in my country, we would be going to the thirteenth floor right now.

That's very interesting, she said, watching the lights of the floor numbers flash on and off, and she imagined that the *bings* made a rhythm, a song.

*Ba ba. Ba ba ba. Ba ba.*

And she put words to it:

*You are Going up now You are . . .*

The *thirteenth* floor, he said, shaking his head. Back in my country that's supposed to be bad luck. Are you superstitious?

Everyone's a little superstitious, she said.

When the elevator reached the twelfth floor, the inner door slowly slid open, like it had no choice, then he slid the outer door open and gestured for her to step out. The hallway was dimly lit by blue lights. On both sides of the elevator, numbered doors receded into black holes.

She walked down the hallway, wondering what her superstition would be, and she wondered what the difference was between a ritual and a superstition. Like how every afternoon before she gets on the train to the city, she makes the sign of the cross. Was that superstition? Did she believe if she *didn't* make the sign of the cross while getting in the train that something bad would happen?

Probably not, so it probably wasn't a superstition but a ritual.

The man took a left at intersecting hallways.

Don't go that way, she said. It's this way.

He looked at the numbers on the wall, 1214–1222.

Oh you're right, he said, and he turned around and followed her.

The door was unlocked. He opened it and let her enter, and he followed behind her. The room was big and clean and well lit, and a flat-screen TV hung on the wall like a painting. There was a Jacuzzi behind glass, large enough for a party.

Nice, he said.

She sat on the bed and looked around, her red purse on her lap.

Something's on your mind, he said. Is everything okay?

When she was a girl, she lived in the city, the fifteenth floor of a building, on an avenue lined by other high-rise buildings as far as the eye could see.

Now she looked up at the black screen of the TV reflecting an image of her sitting on the bed with her red purse in her lap and his shadowy figure pacing the room like he was nervous.

She remembered that their apartment only had one bedroom, so the kids slept in the living room, and their windows looked out onto the side of another building, just a grimy wall.

She opened her red purse to look for something, but then she closed it again.

On the bottom floor of her building there was a man who lived alone. They would never learn his name, but he lived there for as long as they did, probably for a long time before them and probably a long time after they had to move out because the city became too expensive. The man's kitchen window faced the sidewalk on the avenue, and at night when he ate, he had his shutters up and his curtains pulled wide open. Anyone walking by on the sidewalk could just look in, and there he was sitting at the table eating dinner with a glass of purple wine. He seemed to eat pasta or pizza every night, but it was funny to see him, because it was like he didn't care that he was on display. There was a bus stop not five meters away from his window, and all the people lining up for the next bus to arrive could see him right there, but he ate his dinner as if he were completely alone.

He sometimes didn't wear a shirt, and he wasn't fat, but he was thick, and he had a hairy belly. All her childhood in the city he was there, living on floor zero, but the only time she ever saw him was when he ate. She never saw him in the lobby. Never saw him in the elevator or walking down the street or in the grocery store on the corner.

Maybe he didn't have air-conditioning, or maybe he didn't like to run it, but in summer, he would slide open the glass all the way, and you could reach your arm inside and touch him, if you wanted to.

Is something wrong? he asked.

I need to use the bathroom, she said, and she took her red purse and went into the little room, closed the door.

She looked at herself in the mirror, her dyed red hair, matching lips, green eye shadow.

And as she pulled out her lipstick she remembered something. Every spring, when the man started to open the glass, it was for her a sign that summer was coming. It was something she looked forward to, an open window.

Next to her lipstick she put a disc that contained her blush, right next to it, so they were perfectly aligned.

Then her family moved to the provinces, where she still lives.

And in between the lipstick and the blush she put an eyeliner pencil and a book of matches.

To get to the city, she takes a train, and from there a bus and another bus or the *subte*. She wondered if he was still there, or maybe he was dead, because it was ten years ago, and he seemed like an old man, and she was just a kid.

She looked at her face, her lips, her eyes. No, she decided, she was fine, and one by one she put the items back into her purse, lipstick first, then the disk, the pencil, and the matches last.

****

The man pressed the button for the elevator.

When it arrived, he slid open the outer door, and he waited for her to get in, but she didn't get in.

She remembered that the man who ate dinner by the window had a picture on his wall, a painting, nothing fancy or artsy, just a silly painting, and it was framed in this fake gilded gold, like it was a great work of art that should be hanging in a museum.

The elevator started to beep.

It was such a stupid painting. But she looked at it all the time. She looked out for it. She held her breath until she saw it, and then she could breathe again. You could tell that it was a cheap painting.

It was a horse. Or a cow.

Yes, a cow eating grass in a big, green field. Nothing around, just the cow eating grass.

And she realized that if she ever had a superstition, it was that cow, because on days she didn't see it, she thought bad things would happen to her. She would walk the opposite direction out of her building just so she could pass the window and see the cow. The other kids yelled at her, *This way, stupid!* but once she could look in and see the cow, she'd run back to the other kids, all happy and excited.

Her superstition, she realized, was a stupid cow!

The beep seemed to get louder, more urgent. A red light in the elevator was blinking, warning them to get in.

She stepped into the box. He slid closed the outer door, and the inner door slid closed on its own.

He pressed 0.

# A DELICIOUS BURGER

I saw something today that made me really happy, like . . . I don't know, more than anything I ever felt in my life.

She prepared herself. Okay, what did you see today?

He adjusted his belt and sat in an armchair.

She looked at his shoes. The patent leather of the toes reflected the curve of the city. You're going to think it's strange.

Probably, she said, probably very strange.

I don't know, he said, maybe I'm not normal. He smiled and waited to hear her reaction, but she was looking at the glass horse he had on an occasional table, a crystal stallion rising on its hind legs, a prism of colors.

When she was fourteen, a boy won her a horse at the fair.

She liked watching him play the game, which seemed complicated at the time, like it required skill, his fingers flickering, his wrists twirling.

His horse came in first, and he stood up and raised his arms in victory. The carnie handed the boy a copper-colored horse with a saddle, its body positioned as if standing. Posing. It looked like a fine work of art, something from the museum, and the boy handed it to her.

For you, he said, and for the rest of the night she carried it, occasionally petting its little metal head like it was a real horse.

You're really good at that game, she said.

I win every year, he said.

Now she understood that the game required no skill. All you did was pull a pinball-like lever and let the metal ball go free, falling down a slant into one of several little passages, hoping it hits on a high number and your plastic horse moves further toward the finish line than the others.

She couldn't recall what happened to the stupid horse. Or the stupid boy.

Okay, don't think I'm weird, he said. I saw it this afternoon. About one . . . one-thirty.

What did you see? She said *what did you see* with sarcastic excitement, like a teenage girl, even though she was thirty-three, a single mother of an eight-year-old girl.

He was fifty, and he had no job, and all he did all day was read and think and write, and drink a lot of wine. He was usually drunk by five, but he didn't seem drunk now. Maybe he was on coke or pot?

His family owned things—buildings, houses, maybe even the entire building they were in. It was in the center of the city, and his apartment was on the forty-fourth floor. She liked the view. She looked down at his shoes to see it reflected there. Soon, she would have to pick up her daughter from school and then make her dinner. From his place it would take forty-five minutes to drive to her school and then another thirty minutes to their shitty apartment.

I saw a woman walking with a bag of burgers, he said.

Excuse me?

I know, it's weird, he said, but she's this young woman walking out of McDonald's with a bag of food.

So?

Well, I watched her.

What are you saying?

Well, it's obvious she went there to get the food "to go" because she wants to eat it at home or maybe in a park near where she works, but she presumably pays for the food, takes the bag, walks out the doors, onto the sidewalk. She walks . . . I don't know, with a bounce in her step. She's holding that bag of burgers, maybe fries and ketchup inside, and in the other hand she carries a soda in a plastic cup with a straw, and . . . she's happy.

Was she fat?

That has nothing to do with it. It's her face. You could see. Because when you're carrying a bag of burgers, heading toward where you imagine yourself eating them, that could bring more pleasure than actually eating. You know what I mean?

I guess.

She had such a bounce in her step! Such hope . . . It's as if all that matters in the world, in the whole entire world, the only thing that will ever matter is that she has a delicious burger.

It's like . . . he continued, and he stood up and walked around the apartment.

Nothing in the world, nothing, nothing, nothing matters, only the fact that a block away, maybe two blocks away, maybe a few flights of stairs, maybe a few minutes waiting for an elevator, it's like you know for certain you're gunna be eating a delicious burger. But it's more than that!

He was getting worked up.

She was so happy! Just walking with that bag of burgers, not eating them, but *walking* with them. So at peace that it was clear that what mattered most wasn't the burgers themselves but the fact that she *desired* the burgers. It's as if *desire* is what's important, not executing the desire. Not doing what you desire, but desire itself. Does that make sense to you?

No, she said.

# THE THIRD REASON

It was a Tuesday night, a regular evening mass, and there were even fewer people than usual, maybe seven at the most, maybe eight, maybe less, five or six. The stranger walked in late, and you could almost feel winter come in with him. He wore a black coat that fell past his knees, made of material so fine and shiny that it must have cost ten thousand pesos. Under his coat he wore a suit of fine silk perfectly tailored for his body. A gold watch shone on his wrist.

Occasionally, someone walking in the city would stumble inside our doors, tired of alcohol or drugs or a bad relationship. Maybe they hoped to find some sign from God that their life was about to change, and it was obvious that they had never been inside a Catholic church.

Not this rich man. He was a Catholic, all right. He knew when to sit and stand and kneel, and he repeated the prayers without hesitation. Even when Father Flood, who was very old and getting senile, forgot the part about giving each other the sign of peace, the rich man knew it would have been there, and without thinking he shook the hand of the person next to him.

Even though there were millions of people in the city, and hundreds of thousands living in high-rise apartments in Villa Freud, if there was someone new at a weeknight mass, I noticed right away.

But the newcomer I saw that night was so out of place in the sanctuary that it could have been a Sunday evening, when the church was full, and I would have noticed him.

When it was time for the offering, old Martín carried the basket to the front. He was so old he looked like a walking metaphor for death. When he reached the altar, he made the sign of the cross and turned around. He went from row to row, extending the basket for the offering, very slowly. The regulars dropped their coins inside, and I could hear them clinking.

I leaned over and whispered in Father Flood's ear.

"There's three reasons," I said, continuing our conversation from earlier. "One. I'm insufferably neat. Even a drop of water in the sink bothers me like you wouldn't believe. Who could live with that?"

"I see," he said, nodding his head as if he were listening to my confession. Father Flood was in his nineties, and I was in my mid-fifties. I had been helping him with the evening mass for more than twenty years.

Martín finally reached the altar, and he handed me the collection basket. Father Flood prayed over it. When the Eucharist was about to start, I pulled the chalice from the silver box and brought it to him. After the prayers, I was the first one to receive the Body of Christ. I held out my hands, and Father Flood placed the wafer in my palms.

Then we offered the Host to the congregation.

The regulars came up, but the rich man sat during communion. I couldn't make out his face from where I was, because the light came from behind him. Thus from where I stood, he stood in chiaroscuro, but you could tell he was handsome.

After mass, I took the garment from the shoulders of Father Flood. I took the offering, shook the bag, and heard the coins.

At home, I had a new bottle of Chardonnay, and I was eager to get home and drink it. After mass, after everyone had left, I told Father Flood that wine was the second reason. I drink at least a bottle a day, which most people wouldn't understand, but I accept that about myself.

Wine is one of life's pleasures.

Father Flood nodded his head, then he said he wasn't feeling well. He asked me if I would lock up. He said goodnight and went to leave, but before he was able to reach the doorway, I said, "Father, wait!"

I wanted to tell him the third reason, the one that really mattered, but he had a look of nausea on his face, as if he were very sick. He clearly had nothing invested in our conversation, and maybe he'd even forgotten the question he had asked me.

"Do you need anything at the pharmacy?"

"No, no, I'll be fine. I just need rest," he said. "Thank-you. Thank-you." Then he left.

Inside, the church was silent.

Outside I could hear voices, young people yelling, car horns, the "cartoneros" collecting cardboard from the garbage.

The cartoneros, often entire families, went through the streets all night long looking for cardboard. I could hear the squeaky wheels of their carts passing and them yelling to each other.

I looked around Flood's office, but I didn't see any cardboard I could put in front of the church for them.

I sat at Flood's desk.

There was a lamp and a ledger. I dumped the contents of the collection bag onto the desktop.

Then I saw it.

Among all the regular coins and single bills was a roll of hundred-dollar bills, U.S. dollars. I could smell the fresh paper money. It was a thick roll, and in my mind I saw the stranger standing in the pews, light shining on his shoulders.

I wrote the night's total into the ledger, a number that would certainly get the accountant's attention in the morning.

I walked across the room and opened the door to the cabinet. From a drawer I pulled out a wooden box with a tiny lock. I put the key inside the lock and turned it. The box opened. I pushed the money inside and closed the lid. I locked the box and put it back in the drawer.

I turned off the lights.

The only light in the empty nave came from the street, the shadows of the empty pews stretching out on the walls. I walked onto the altar, past the statues. I turned around, looked up at the statue of our Holy Mother. *Thanks to the Mother*, I said, making the sign of the cross, and I walked down the aisle. I could hear my footsteps. My shadow rose up the walls. I could hear the city, car horns and braking buses, squeaky wheels. When I reached the huge doors, I turned around, faced the altar, and made the sign of the cross again.

I went out and locked the doors of the church. I walked down the church steps onto the sidewalk.

It was a cold night, enough so that the cafés had no tables on the sidewalks. Inside they were full. The women walking home from work had themselves wrapped in coats and scarves. I walked through the streets, past more cafés and newsstands and flower vendors and people waiting for buses or descending into the underground.

I reached my street and stopped to look at the parrilla on the corner. I knew they served good steaks and my favorite Malbec. And I liked the waiter there. He was a professional Buenos Aires waiter, a man in his fifties, always wore a bow tie and vest, and he served with a flourish, the way he opened the wine, twirled the cork in his fingers before setting it in front of you to inspect. He cut the steak with knife and fork, making a beat the way the metal tapped the plate.

And as he did all this, he never said anything to me, but he had a friendly look on his face, and you could tell that he was just as much at peace as I was. We just left each other in peace, no need to feel like we had to say something.

And those moments, when dinner was about to arrive, when he unfolded my napkin, he was like a magician! He would pull the napkin from its folded triangle on the table and flick his wrist, the napkin blurring and twisting like a flag. Then he placed the napkin next to my plate, and the triangle became a flower, the napkin spreading out its white petals.

# PART THREE

# RUNNING THROUGH A MUSEUM

## One

"Which one do you want?" I asked Marianne as we sat in the museum café, the LA Getty on the 405. She was seventeen years old.

"The Fond Story," she said.

"Aw, that old thing?" I said.

"Tell me the Fond Story. Please, Daddy!"

"Again?"

"I'm *fond* of it."

"Where do you want me to start? The school?"

"No, the fast train."

"Okay, Anton and I . . ."

"The German artist."

"We were on our way to meet the girls in Marseilles."

"The *women*, Dad. You mean the *women*. Not *girls*."

"You know what I mean," I said.

"I *do* know what you mean. You mean *girls*. But they're not girls."

"Do you want to hear the story?"

"Proceed."

"So we were going to meet your mom and her sister, and then we would take the train to Barcelona and spend four days. Anton was going be the companion to your mom's little sister, your aunt Sonia-Assis, who was quite young, eighteen or nineteen."

"On the train to meet them Anton slept most of the way, but I couldn't sleep on high- speed trains."

"Scary?"

"No, it's . . . sad. The greatest pleasure of a train is looking out the window, seeing things slowly pass, and if something grabs your attention, you can look at it from several angles as the train slowly moves by. You can really *see* it, but if the train is going too fast, it flattens the image and the Lorentz contraction kicks in and everything looks smaller and it blurs so quickly you can't get a good look, and that's kind of sad."

"I don't get it."

"Imagine you're running through a museum. I mean, really running. Running for your life."

"Why would I do that?"

"I don't know. Someone's chasing you."

"Who?"

"Someone who wants to hurt you. Maybe wants you dead. You're running for your life through the museum. The paintings are blurs, swirls of color and shape, a face, a shoulder, and even if something strikes you, you can't stop and stand before it. You can't take it in because you have to run."

"Who would want to hurt me in a museum? That's stupid."

"Are we really using that word again? You're acting like a brat."

"Hmm, funny," she said as if thinking, even putting a finger on her chin like a thinker. "Whenever I have my own opinion, I'm a brat. If I have *your* opinion, I'm a good girl."

"I'm just saying, it's the image, running through the museum, not the reason."

"How can you separate the image from the meaning?"

"Just shut up, please. I'm sitting by a window on a high-speed train and I feel like I'm running through a museum."

"But even if the train is fast, you can still see what's outside. The Lorentz contraction isn't measurable unless the train is going close to the speed of light. You would still see everything—a field of sunflowers, a horse eating grass!"

I smiled, took a drink of my wine, looked at her with happy eyes.

"What?" she said.

"Nothing," I said. "I'm just proud of you is all."

Her teenager kicked in, and she rolled her eyes and said, "Whatever."

"Okay, when the train passes through a town, and the walls are too close. You see nothing but blur and watered-down shapes. What if I saw something that struck me and I wanted to look at it longer? Anyway, the point is, I couldn't sleep, so I decided to read *that* book."

"*Lives of the Saints*?" she guessed.

"Unlikely," I said.

"*The Satanic Verses*?"

## Two

You know how some people say a single book changed their lives? I never believed it. I thought that one book could *encourage* you to go in the direction in which you're already heading, but a book couldn't change you.

But this one did.

But here's the weird thing:

I don't remember the book. I don't remember the title, what it was about, whether or not it was a novel or poems or nonfiction. I don't even remember the language—English, French, or Spanish.

From the first time I told Marianne about it, she didn't believe a book could be so important and yet I could forget all about it. "Impossible," she said, but I tried to explain that it was the *reading* of the book, the entering into the glow. *That* was what changed me. The Glow. Every book has a glow. Yes, God may very well be in the details, but He/She/They is not trapped inside them.

Even if I can never go back inside, I've been there.

Reading a book you'll forget is like visiting a foreign city in your youth. You forget the details in your later years, but the experience still *was*. It still changed you.

But Marianne didn't believe it, and she always fought me. She said for me to have any credibility, I would need to know the name. Anytime the book came up in conversation, she tried to coach me on recalling the title, reciting a random list of books in all three of her languages, her mom's French, my Spanish, and our English.

"*The Death of Time*? *The Fabric of Reality*? *The Iceworker Sings*?"

"No. No."

"Something by Shakespeare?"

"I don't remember."

"*Le rouge et le noir?*"

"*Á la recherche du temps perdu?*"

"No! Just stop being so stubborn!"

"Ok, what do you remember *about* the book?" she'd challenge.

But when I try to remember the slightest detail, I sometimes see shapes and light and think I'm close to remembering a stone building with broken windows, or a wall on the edge of the sea, or a cat cleaning itself in a window, but then those images fade into all the other times I have known those images, and I can't get back inside the glow.

## Three

I stood up, grabbed my backpack, and walked to the café car. I ordered a coffee and sat on a stool.

I liked the coffee. It tasted good.

"But what about the book?" she asked, bringing me back to the Getty Museum café.

"That comes later," I said.

"You used to be good at telling stories," she said.

"You used to be good at listening to them," I said.

So some teenage girls came into the car. They ordered in English and took a seat at a table near me. They were Americans, and one of them said, "That was so not cool." She said "so" with two syllables, and the others agreed. "Natalie is being such a bitch!"

Then an Arabic couple walked in, a young man and a woman all covered in black, including most of her face. Her eyes in all that darkness were so bright, so beautiful.

They ordered in French.

I looked out the window. Something orange-brown blurred by, but I didn't know what it was, perhaps a stone building or a pile of rocks. I remember a sort of bluish color swirled into the rest of the image.

I wanted to kill time.

I opened my backpack and pulled out . . .

"The book!" Marianne said, as if to say, *Finally!*

"A pen and a pad."

I sketched the Arab couple near the window. I used crosshatch shading for the woman's hijab. Out the train window behind them I sketched rolling hills and a stone building and a crescent moon against the sky. The man is looking out the window, but we see her face in profile. I tried to make her eyes look like she was dreaming.

I sketched the boy who worked the café, wiping the counter. I put a lot of anger into his eyes. Behind him, I sketched in the shelves, the refrigerators, the espresso machine, the advertisements.

I sketched the teenage girls, laughing, whispering over the table to each other. I used minimal details for their faces, mostly eyes and mouths to capture their characters, but with just a few suggestive lines for their noses, chins, eyebrows.

Two old men came in, one leading the other, who had a white cane, and I sketched the man with the cane, but I took him out of the train and had him walking along an empty street lined by Gothic buildings and streetlamps shaped like candles. I imagined walking with him on an ordinary night in the city, having a conversation.

The swish of the pen made a quick back-and-forth rhythm like the needle on a polygraph, and I must have been there awhile, because people came and went. I love the feel of a pen sliding across a white page. The strokes swish and curve, and as the pen goes faster and faster I sometimes find images on the paper that I had little to do with, as if all I had to do was submit my hand.

"God is soooo boring!" Marianne interrupted.

"What?" and I was back in the museum. I took a drink of my wine.

"You said God is in the details. Well if that's true, with all the details you're telling me, God's a pretty boring guy. Just get to the Fond."

"I'm getting there."

Anton joined me in the café car.

"How's the coffee?" he asked.

"Not bad," I said.

"But you're American," he said. "You drink Folgers."

I shrugged my shoulders.

He went to get coffee and returned.

"May I?" he asked indicating my drawings, and I nodded.

He looked through them. He picked up the one with the Arab couple, and he examined the detail.

"Is she happy?"

"Maybe," I said.

"I hope you weren't offended by my 'American' comment," he said.

"Not at all," I said. "Besides, I'm not really an American. At least not the stereotype."

"Yes, that's right," he nodded. "You are a Chicano."

"¡Con safos y qué!" I said.

"Sonia wants to pose for me," he said. "It was her idea."

"Does she know how abstract you are? She'll end up a twisted wire."

"What fine wire that would be!"

Anton took two tiny coffee straws that were lying on the table, and he started to twist them into shapes. He made little knots that could have been Sonia-Assis or barbed wire. Or maybe it was nothing, but by the tender look on his face as he twisted the plastic you could tell it was something.

## Four

I don't remember much about the first time I saw Marseilles, so my details may not be exact, but I remember the train station seemed to be built on a giant white rock, like a huge structure from the Roman days.

The steps descended down into the city, onto a wide avenue with Paris-style buildings that reached all the way to the horizon. The rooftops of the city spread all around, as far as the mountains. In the distance, there was what looked like a castle on a hill.

"What a city!" said Anton.

"You ever been here before?" I asked.

"Never," he said.

We continued to look around, awed by the city and the expanse of mountains miles away. "Do you see the ladies?" Anton said, looking around.

The sun was intense, hot, dry. It burnt my face.

"I'll go look on the other side," I said.

I saw a clock hanging on a white wall, a white face with thick metal hands. I thought of my father. It was 10:10. I walked toward it. I saw her. She stood beneath the clock, inside a triangle of white suitcases. When she saw me, she crossed her arms and shook her head in disappointment.

"What?" I asked.

"I still can't believe I'm dating an American."

"Chicano," I said.

"Whatever," she said.

## Five

On the train, the four of us were happy. I cuddled with Amelle, brought in her smell, taking deep breaths through my nose, and I could tell she was a bit irritated by it, because she wasn't an affectionate person. She was more comfortable with sex than she was with affection, and even when we walked through a city or a park she couldn't hold hands for very long. She was also often in a foul, ironic mood, and we fought a lot, but we made up just as passionately. I told myself we would never make it past my year at the art school, that I would go back to LA and live out the rest of my life and never see her again, but I was falling in love with her in spite of myself.

Anton and Sonia were in the seats facing us, cuddled up together, asleep. "That's cool of your sister to come," I said. "I hope she kind of likes him."

"What?" she asked, like I was an idiot.

"They seem to really like each other."

"You are sounding very ignorant," she said.

"No, I think he really likes her," I said.

"What are you talking about?"

"How Sonia-Assis came for our sake, so we could do this."

"For us? No, she didn't do it for us. We're doing it for *them*."

She indicated *them* with her head. Sonia and Anton were still asleep, and by the light on their faces I could see now that they were in love.

"Wait a minute. Are you saying that we're going away together for their sake?" I asked.

"If it were just us, we'd share a room, wouldn't we? Think about it."

"Did you go out with me just so your sister could meet Anton?"

"At first, yes. I knew you were mates."

"Mates? What, are you British now?"

"He was your friend."

"That's the *only* reason you went out with me?"

"At first, Victor, but since that time I have become fond of you."

"*Fond*?"

I think I love you, I wanted to say, but all I could do was utter incredulously, "*Fond*? You're *fond* of me?"

## Six

I didn't talk to her for the rest of the ride, but then I couldn't help it, I muttered the word "fond" as if it were ugly and mean.

"That is all, Victor!" she said. She told me (in French) that her English wasn't that good and I should understand that, and I should let her words be her words and try not to make them mine.

She pulled out a book and started to read. It was in Arabic.

I didn't even understand the alphabet. To me it looked like some secret, ancient text.

## Seven

When Anton and I brought in our bags, he was happy, singing.

He opened the window, which looked out onto another window across the narrow alley, and at the end of the path was the green neon cross of a pharmacy.

I closed the window.

"What's the matter?" he asked.

"Nothing," I said.

I remember the girls knocked on the door, ready to go to dinner, but I told them I was just going to stay in the room, that I was tired.

"Good for you!" said Amelle.

I remember her slamming the door on her way out.

"I'm not FOND of Spanish food," I yelled.

"Then go back to your country!" she yelled.

## Eight

My memory blurs here.

I know I spent hours alone in that room. It was dark outside, and I remember reaching over a lamp to turn on the light. I might have heard cathedral bells outside announcing the hours, each *bong!* telling me I was a fool, "a creature driven by vanity." I think I remember grabbing the book from my backpack. Or maybe it was in my messenger's bag. I remember opening the book. But that's it. That's all I remember.

I must have been inside that book for a long time, but I don't remember details, only light, like when you wake up from a dream about a city or a river or a meadow, you don't remember what you were seeing and try to recall the image, but all you see is light.

Less than a year later, when Amelle was pregnant with our daughter, we were shopping for vegetables in an open market. She said, "I love the smell of green things." She held greens to her nose, maybe spinach, maybe broccoli, maybe chard, I don't remember.

I don't remember what outdoor market it was or what city we were in, just me and her walking in the market. Many of my memories of her are made up of blurry scenes, streams of swirls and shapes and colors, like running in a museum.

The vendors are fading into black, and we are walking. Amelle's pregnant.

I think I saw an old Sikh man sitting on a worn blanket, but I don't know if I'm creating him or if he was really there. He's selling headlights for cars, or was that a flea market in Fresno when I was a teenager?

I see a perfume vendor in a white straw hat with a microphone clipped to the lapel of his ice cream suit announcing in French the great deals.

I see Amelle carrying a bag of ripe green things, which she keeps smelling. Her eye catches a red scarf hanging from a booth. I see two tiny red scarfs shining in her eyes. She says, *How pretty.* I see a light come on beneath our feet.

"Where are we?" she asks.

"*¿La ciudad y los perros?*" Marianne asked.

"No."

"*¿La vida es sueño?*"

"No, no. That's not it," I said, but she was persistent and wanted to know.

"You're losing focus, Dad. Where are you?"

"Telling you the Fond Story."

"*Niebla? ¿Dime quien soy?*"

"Is that a title or a question?"

"All I got to say is . . ." Marianne said, and she leaned into me and practically yelled, "My Arab-tina ass!"

"What are you talking about?"

"This is bullshit, Dad! How can you forget a book so important to you? I don't buy it. You remember what's important to you. You remember!"

And she was really mad at me. I could see it in her eyes, like she was about to cry.

"What's wrong, honey?" I said.

"Just finish the story," she said.

## Nine

There is no ending.

I was in the room and the cathedral or church or from some place the bells were ringing, *bongs* separated by seconds. I remember I would end up counting eleven *bongs*. That number is certain.

Eleven.

But in between those *bongs*, maybe on the third or fourth one, I realized what she had meant by saying that she didn't speak English very well.

She meant that I understood the subtle differences in English between words like "fond" and "like" better than she did.

What does "fond" mean to her?

On another *bong*, maybe the eighth or ninth, I put down the book.

On the last *bong*, number eleven, I thought that maybe she loved me too.

I went out into the city and searched for her. I walked through narrow alleys of the Gothic neighborhood, through shaded plazas, through entrances in walls. Along Las Ramblas I looked into cafés and walked into the dim recesses of bars. I walked along the pier where dark yachts swayed in the harbor.

I went back to the hotel to check if she had returned or left a message for me. Nothing.

I wandered into a city park, a place of trees and plants and stone paths surrounded by a tall, stone wall. Once I entered the gates, it occurred to me that this was where I would find her. The feeling was so strong that it left no room for doubt.

Giant poplars lined the path, moonlight through the leaves. I thought I saw her. She appeared at the vanishing point of the path, a tiny silhouette so far away that I couldn't tell if she was coming toward me or walking away. I knew it was her. I ran. I yelled her name and ran.

Bushes and trees swirled by like brushstrokes. Her figure turned off the path and disappeared into a garden, so I left the path.

A man appeared in chiaroscuro, coming out of the light. He carried a rifle.

A badge shone on his chest. He looked at me with white eyes, and I asked him in Spanish if he had seen her, describing her. He said the park was closed. I had to leave, he said.

Marianne stood up to leave.

"Where are you going?" I asked.

"Back inside," she said. "I want to see the paintings."

A train whistle sounded. I heard voices in the distance, a scream, laughter, car on a highway, a passing jet, a foghorn from the ocean.

# YI VUT LO PURKE

The language she spoke is tough to master, not only because it has masculine and feminine nouns and verbs, like Spanish and French, but also because a word changes not only according to the person uttering it, but also to myriad factors like weather, for example, or time of day.

They say the Inuit have fifty words for "snow," but in her language they have more than three thousand!

Or any noun, like the word "park." I don't remember an exact example. I forget what little I knew of the language, but say that the raw form of the noun "park" was *lo puc*, "the park."

The noun in *that* particular form implies a park *in the morning*. *Yi vu lo parc* would mean, "I want to go to the park (in the morning)." If you're a woman, however, you would say *Yi vut lo purke* because both the verb and the noun change according to who's speaking. In the afternoon, a man would say, *Yi vi lo park*, "I want to go to the park (in the afternoon)," whereas a woman would say, *Yi vutte lo pakka*. If you were transgender you would say *peurk* or *puerk*, according to the gender with which you identify most; if you do not lean toward one or the other, the word is *püek*.

The root word for "park (at night)" is *pawk*, but there is no word for "park late at night," that is, after midnight, because if I recall correctly, she told me that after midnight the park gates are shut. The lights blink off, and no one can enter into the garden until sunrise. The garden at night is for spirits and jinn.

She said they have more than 35,000 conjugations of a single verb, and because they are so specific, a single verb can express myriad human experiences or fit any individual's unique reason for talking. I don't remember the exact details, so let's make up a word, just as an example. Say that one rainy day, a foreign man is glowing with desire, and he wants to go to the park (at night) with his lady friend, but he needs to put on his shoes, the ones he recently bought (less than three days before) in an open-air market that day he handed the man his money and looked across the street and thought he saw his dead brother sitting on a stone bench looking down at his reflection in a pond, he would say, *Yi vutu loko pakkutka*, unless there were ducks in the pond.

This particular modification of the noun "park," *pakkutka*, contains all the above detail, all of it, down to the dead brother, for if he saw a living brother, it would be *pakuutka*.

*If* the brother was younger.

If he was older, it would be *pakuitka*.

She told me that because there are so many diverse sounds and rhythms, their language comes closer than any other to eliminating the separation between what we want to express and the expression itself. It's as close as you can get to pre-Tower babel.

Poets are useless in her language.

I learned a few words while we were there for two weeks visiting her family, very basic things, but after decades of not using it, I lost it all. I used to know how to say "good-bye" and "thank-you" and "where's the toilet," and I could even walk into a store in the evening and ask for a cold bottle of water, but I don't remember any of the words now. I don't know how to say "bottle." I don't remember how to say "thank-you." I don't know how to say "good-bye."

I heard that no matter how long a nonnative speaker studies the language, and even if he or she knows all the conjugations, when he or she attempts to pronounce the words, his or her foreign accent is disturbingly strong to native speakers. They cover their ears when foreigners speak their language because it's a horrible sound, like tin dragged across cement, vicious dogs fighting to the death, babies screaming in an elevator. Whenever I tried to speak her language, she would say, "Please speak English only," even though it sometimes hurt my feelings.

They have so many odd sounds and rhythms and intonations, so many ways of using their tongue and teeth and saliva, so many pitches and tones, that I don't think it could ever be mastered by a foreigner.

For example:

Let's say a man is walking through an open-air market with his partner. He smells fish and wet onions—and he's walking through shouting and salty goods, and he looks at the woman, and she has black hair and black eyes, and he knows they are meant to be together.

She stops and looks at a booth of tomatoes piled high as the sea, and she turns around and says to him with a smile, "I love . . ."

And he thinks she's going to say *you*, I love *you*, but she says, . . . "the smell of red." And she sniffs a tomato as she holds it in her palms.

He's hurt, because he already told her several times that he loves her, and all she does is squeeze his hand or pretend she didn't hear it. Now she asks, "What do you want to do?" And he says he wants to go to the park and she tells him it's almost midnight and the park gates will be shut and they could be stuck in there all night with the jinn and he says that wouldn't be so bad, but really, he keeps saying to himself, *She doesn't love you, go back to your country.*

Even if he learned how to say all this, that he wants to go to the park (in these circumstances), the words would be, for example, *Yu Vilio Entp2artokulo*, but he wouldn't be able to pronounce it.

His lips and tongue would have to twist and deform into sounds impossible for him. The conjugation of the verb "to go" itself could be *Whaaaakrakkrahagahaghahjdotmiiiiiiahhh!*

The conjugation of "to want" could be *Ahghhhrhrhrhrhrhhrhr-hryutyytr!*

To express his desire, he would need to call out, *Urrhgekskehekjjr-rrkkrahagahaghahjdotmdjdjjd lsldllslssstkhthithjthtofdjnsikdAhaagh aaahaaahraaahaaaraaahaaaraahaa . . .*

# A DEATH OF TIME

"Their most popular genre of painting is Still Lives," I said. "You know?"

"Of course," Marianne said. "Cherries in a white bowl, sunflowers in a vase, a dead rabbit hanging from a hook."

"Right! To your mom's people, Still Lives have so much meaning that the name they give them is worth considering. In Spanish we say, *naturaleza muerta*, Dead Nature, and in French they say . . ."

She interrupted, "*We* say, *nature morte.*"

"Yes, which literally translated also means Dead Nature. It makes sense. But in English we say Still Lives, and I find it funny that you can also read it as 'still *lives*,' that is, 'still *living*.' Isn't that a cool linguistic coincidence?"

"That's stupid," she said.

"But think about it. If the object represented in the painting, the apple or the pipe, even if it doesn't exist anymore, even if the fruit has long rotted, it still *lives*."

"Anyway, you were talking about Mom's language."

"Right. Right. In *their* language, 'a Still Life' painting literally translated into English would be something like 'a Death of Time' painting."

"A Death of Time? You're a liar. I took Arabic last summer. I don't remember hearing about that."

"I'm not talking Arabic. If I remember correctly, in Arabic, a Still Life painting is *yazalu, taswir zaytiin*. Your mom's people were from

Morocco, yes, but before that, they came from a distant island to the east, where they spoke one of the world's rarest and most difficult languages."

"This is stupid. Mom wasn't Wonder Woman."

"Anyway, in their language, the object painted, a cracked wine-glass, a skull on a desk, exists not only in the work but in the thoughts of the observers, in the realm of imagination, which they believe is just as real as matter. So when you look at a painting, you kill time. Clocks quit clicking and the dead rabbit lives."

"What about portraits?" she asked. "If a painter captures a human subject, does that mean that time stops and the person lives?"

"Wow. That's a good question."

"Does the Mona Lisa walk the halls of the Louvre at night when no one's around?"

"Maybe."

"Because if so," she said. "Mom is everywhere. How many times have you painted her?"

"I couldn't count."

"But according to you, according to *her* people, she's not dead. Time stopped and she's right here. Right now."

We both looked at the window, where a curtain slightly moved, and I got goose bumps. Amelle stood there, her arms crossed, looking back and forth at both of us.

She was the age she was when she died.

"Your father's a liar," she said. "I'm one hundred percent Arab-Berber."

"I knew it," said Marianne. "A Death of Time my ass!"

They both said it together, looking right at me, "That's so stupid!"

# A YOUNG CITY

The girls and boys who work the cafés and bars and tourist shops are just that, girls and boys, some of them having barely entered their teens.

The passersby in the city squares, the people who populate the tables of outdoor cafés, the tourists snapping pictures of statues are all in their teens or twenties, young and good-looking and disposed to laugh. The girls are beautiful, their hair long and shiny and their skin smooth and their bodies firm and tall, and all the boys are handsome and svelte and strong.

On the city's underground train, young people pile into the cars like college kids on a dare, and they don't mind at the height of rush hour that they must press their bodies into each other. Oftentimes a girl getting on the train alone at one stop might get off at another stop with a boy on her arm.

Coupling is encouraged and common.

One night, a foreigner comes into the city on his way to another city, and seeing and feeling the sensuality in the air, he decides to stay the night in one of the downtown hotels.

The nightlife there is unbelievable. People dress up in sexy clothes and they drink and laugh, and the foreign man has to push through the town square like he's walking through a rock concert, hoping to make a connection, to meet someone.

But he doesn't speak the language, and the first night he has no luck.

The next day, however, on the subway, the foreigner gets on the train. There are no seats left, so he holds onto the bar above his head. The train jiggles him around like a puppet. He sees a girl sitting across from him. She has long red hair and gray eyes, and when she sees the foreigner jiggling with the train, she smiles.

This could be the one, he thinks, and he smiles back.

She bites her young, plump lips, and she practically bats her eyelashes at him, like a girl flirting in a cartoon. He knows he has found her.

The foreigner now notices that there is a boy sitting next to her, talking to her, but she cannot seem to take her eyes off the foreigner. She ignores the boy. The foreigner wants to talk to her before the next stop, for any stop could be hers, and if the doors slide open and she steps out into the bustle of the city, he might lose her forever. He has no time to gamble with fate. He knows this.

The boy sitting next to the girl touches the back of her neck, but she pushes him away and continues to give her eyes to the foreigner. Her face is soft and warm.

He acts.

He walks toward the girl, stumbles with the movement of the car, and she perks up. The boy next to her is clueless, only seems to notice the girl.

When the foreigner reaches the pretty girl, she elbows the boy to get away.

She admonishes the boy in her language. The boy looks up at the foreigner and stands up. He says in the foreigner's language, *Please, sir. Take my seat. You must sit.*

The girl is looking at the boy, and she smiles at him, proud at him for giving his seat to the old man.

# I DID LIKE RICKY

BUENOS AIRES, 2005

I spent a year in Palermo, on Calle Borges, writing a novel about a man and his daughter. I was going to call it *Your Daughters Are Looking at the Moon*, but I never did anything with it, and I think it's still somewhere in The Wall'.

But I wrote all day, and I read books by the antepasados whom I thought would guide me into the landscape of my fiction, Baudelaire, Lorca, Poe.

At night, when I wasn't working, I became restless.

I left my building and walked along the spine of Borges into the commotion of Plaza Italia, as if searching for something.

I stumbled into cafés for a beer and a shot, and I used the toilets to blast *merca* into my nose, and after what must have been a few hours—only sparse images stay with me now: a streetlight slashing the face of an old man, a woman dressed in white yelling at the dead—I ended up on the stoned streets of San Telmo.

At the corner beneath the full moon and a youth hostel, the windows of a café pounded with rock music and desire, so I went in.

It was packed with young Europeans and Americans, the conversations mixing languages and tones like a flock of geese, and the scent of patchouli oil was thick enough to slice and eat.

Some of the patrons had their giant backpacks next to their table, as if they would continue their journey after a beer or two.

I ordered a Quilmes and stood invisible in the dark corner, drunk, watching the people have fun, and I got sad. I said to myself, *Just go back to your country!*

I remembered my brother Ricky in his twenties, a beautiful boy, but shy, and when he got drunk at a bar, he took off his shirt and flirted with women.

He looked like a Native American hunk in the velvet paintings white people buy at tourist markets, his chest of polished wood and his long, black hair shiny like a model in a shampoo commercial. All the white girls wanted to touch his pecs and run their fingers through his hair.

I was forty-three now, and maybe I was just lonely, but a voice whispered to me, *Do like Ricky and take off your shirt.*

So I did.

I did like Ricky and I took off my shirt.

And when I took off my shirt, I wandered through the tables, introducing myself in three languages, shaking hands, kissing cheeks, telling my name,

*I am . . . Me llamo . . . Je suis . . .*

I worked the room like a king.

And all the people saw my jiggling man-boobs and the blubber hanging over my belt. And all the people could see the black-widow-spider-legs-of-hair on my chest.

And all the people watched me walk to them, Quilmes in hand, smiles and smiles. Crazy American, they said. Crazy Mexican, they said.

Crazy Chicano! I yelled.

# EVERY BOOK IS A WORMHOLE

Hector's mom and dad were fighting again, so he turned off the TV, grabbed a stack of books, and went to his room. He closed the door and sat in his yellow chair by the window. The chair was old and wobbly, and it used to belong to his grandmother, and he liked the way it creaked back and forth as he read. He decided to read the book about an elephant named Bigger.

He randomly opened the pages and started where Bigger was running, because hunters were chasing him. He was trying to reach the part of the plain where an elephant can hide in the water. Hector read awhile and then put down that book and picked up the one about the bunny who hated carrots and opened it at a random page. Horace had ordered a pizza, and he couldn't wait for it to arrive, so he was pacing around the rabbit hole, imagining himself already eating the pizza, when he looked across the grass and saw his sisters walking toward him.

Hector picked up book about a girl named Quark, and he landed on the page where she was flying through the futuristic city, swerving in and out of glass buildings, in a galaxy far away.

He loved to read, because everything disappeared: his parents yelling, his sister complaining, dogs fighting, police sirens getting closer. Out his window it always sounded like a war going on, but when he was reading, the walls of his bedroom disappeared.

Even the words in the book disappeared, and he forgot he was reading. The story played like a video game, as if he were there, and it was in 4D, because he could smell things, lemons, bananas, a hot pizza.

He liked running through jungles, swerving through tall buildings in a flying saucer, diving into rabbit holes.

He liked to reread books, because every time he went back into those worlds he saw things he hadn't seen before.

Now, he was reading the book with Quark, a girl his age, nine years old. She was standing on a hill overlooking the lights of her city. The buildings were made of glass, and cars with no wheels flew through the air like tiny spaceships. Streetlights didn't hang on poles but flew around wherever they were needed, following people if they needed light.

Hector imagined himself standing next to the girl in the story. Her name was *R%7G*/eqxz*, but everyone called her Quark, especially humans, because they couldn't pronounce her name.

Quark was shaped like a human girl, but she had blue wings coming out of her back. She also had three eyes, and this time, reading the story, Hector noticed for the first time that only her outer two eyes reflected the lights of the city. The third eye was the same color as the other two, and the eyeball could move around and look at things, but it had no tiny reflection in it.

Throughout the city, Quark's species lived with humans, side-by-side in peace for the first time, ever. The city was the happiest place in all the galaxies because everyone got along.

For now.

Hector knew what was about to happen, but at this point in the book, Quark had no idea, and she was happy. She was looking out over the city, her heart content. "This is beautiful," she said. The lights of the city gleamed in two of her three eyes.

He was right there with her, looking over the city, and it felt so real. Quark looked at Hector, right at him, and she smiled.

"Isn't the city pretty?" she asked.

"That was weird," said Hector, putting down his book. "How did she see me?"

Hector's sister opened the door and told Hector it was time to eat. "I'm not hungry," he said.

"Me either. Besides. Guess what we're having? Again?"

"Quesadillas?" said Hector, and his sister closed the door.

During recess at school, Hector found a spot under a fruitless mulberry tree, and he opened the book with Quark, but she didn't seem to notice him this time. She was crying about what was happening to her beautiful city. He was merely an observer, could do nothing, but then later on that day, when he was on lunch break, it happened again.

While kids screamed out their games and a police helicopter flew overhead, he opened the book about the bunny who hated carrots.

Unlike the other bunnies, Horace didn't have big front teeth. His ears were so big and floppy that they dragged on the ground and got dirty at the tips. When his father came home with a basket of carrots as orange as hope, all the other little bunnies got excited and ran around in spins and twirls, flickering their little black noses, but not Horace. He said, "Carrots again? Can't we have cheese pizza?"

He loved cheese pizza more than anything. The other bunnies teased him, because bunnies shouldn't like cheese, or pizza, but Horace hated carrots. He could eat tacos, salads, spaghetti, but he hated carrots.

"You're a bunny," said his mother. "Hating carrots is like hating who you are."

When Horace snuck into the tall grass to eat a slice, Hector was watching him eat, and he imagined himself there. He imagined he could smell the pizza.

He could hear the chewing.

Horace turned around and said right to Hector, "It's mozzarella. Want a bite?"

Hector fell out of the book, back into the schoolyard, underneath the fruitless mulberry tree.

How did that happen? he wondered.

He picked up the book and reentered the story. Horace was still there. "Do you like pizza?" he asked Hector.

"I love pizza," Hector said.

In class one day while Miss Pickles was talking about numbers, Hector snuck out his book and started to read.

Quark was swerving through the tall buildings with her great wings, swirling through the air like an angel. When she saw Hector standing on the hill, she flew up to him and stood right next to him.

"Hi. Want to fly with me?"

"You can see me?" he asked.

"Can *you* see me?"

"Yes! As if you were real."

"Duh. I *am* real," she said, looking him up and down. "You look like a 'real' human." She turned around and offered her back. "Jump on. Like a piggyback ride."

"Are you sure?" Hector asked. "I'm pretty heavy."

"I'm pretty strong," said Quark.

So he jumped on, and she flew into the sky!

Hector could feel the cool air on his cheeks, and he could see for miles and miles, the city stretching all the way to the blue sea and seven full moons shining like planets. She swerved around the moons like a witch on a broom, and he laughed and laughed.

"Do you think math is funny, Hector?" Miss Pickles asked.

"No, Miss. I just thought of something. That's all."

"Well, you have to pay attention, okay?" Hector nodded.

The girl in front of him giggled.

The teacher wrote a bunch of numbers on the board, which to him looked like some secret language he'd never learn, and he opened the book and went back inside the story.

Quark and he were sitting on the top of the city's tallest building. Across from them was a giant video screen of a toothpaste commercial, a little boy of Quark's species happily brushing his teeth, which for them were pointed like fangs.

"Quark? Can I ask you a question?" asked Hector.

"Sure. What do you want to know?"

"Why doesn't your third eye have a reflection in it?"

"I see different things with it," she said. "It's not like the other two."

"What do you see?"

She looked at him and said softly, "I see you."

The fighting got worse. They called each other names and yelled so loud that the police were called and took them both aside to talk about what the problem was, both of them arguing over the shoulders of the policemen like a scene from *Cops*.

After school, instead of going straight home, Hector went to the neighborhood library. He found a tiny wooden chair near a window, and he pulled the string on the lamp and read in his own circle of light.

Horace was being picked on by other bunnies.

They were surrounding him, calling him "big ears" and "pizza breath." They were throwing carrots at him, and Horace was pleading for them to stop. Hector moved through the bunnies and went to help his friend.

"What do I do? They all hate me."

"Let them try the pizza," Hector said.

"What do you mean?"

"I've read this story a zillion times," Hector said. "All you have to do is let them taste the pizza, and they'll see for themselves how delicious it is and that being different is okay!"

So Hector and Horace handed out slices of pizza to all the little bunnies.

They didn't want to try it until Frankie, a chubby little bunny, said, "Why not?" and he took a bite.

Everyone watched him as he chewed.

His eyes went wide. A grin spread across this face. "Frankie likes it!" the bunnies exclaimed.

"It's delicious!" yelled the chubby bunny.

All the bunnies cheered and tried the pizza. Some didn't like it, some did. "Come on," said Hector. "Let's get out of here."

"Where to?"

"You want to meet my friend Quark? She's really cool."

"Yeah! Let's go!"

"Young man!! Young man!!"

It was the librarian. "I told you! The library is closed. You have to go home."

"Oh, sorry," Hector said, and he put his books in the bag and left for home.

In class one day, Hector opened the book about Bigger, the young elephant. In this scene he was running from poachers, who wanted to kill him and take his tusks, which they could sell for a lot of money.

Bigger was running through the plains, pounding the earth. He was trying to reach a place he knew with tall trees and a lake where the elephants drank and took baths.

But now it was deserted. He was very frightened.

He found a cluster of skinny trees, and he stayed there, breathing hard from running. He could hear the rumbles of the trucks in the distance. "He's in the trees!" someone yelled.

The baby elephant looked at Hector and said, "What should I do?"

"Don't worry," Hector said. "I read this story! Follow me."

"Hector?" yelled Miss Pickles. "What's the answer?"

"The mud. He has to hide in the mud."

The class was silent, and as they looked at Hector, he suddenly realized where he was. His face turned red.

They all laughed. The girl in front of him said, "You're a weirdo!"

"What is the answer to the problem on the board?" asked Miss Pickles.

"I don't know," he said.

"See me after class," she said.

"Hector, why are your grades so bad? You're such a smart kid."

He shrugged. He wanted to get back to Bigger.

"Are you spending too much time watching TV?" she asked.

"I don't watch TV," he said.

"Well, what do you do with all your time?"

"Read."

"What do you read?"

Hector opened his school bag and took out some books. "This is what I'm reading now."

She looked at the stack and said, "All those chapter books?"

"I like reading," he said.

"Do you learn anything?"

He shrugged his shoulders. "I just like them," he said.

She walked to her desk, opened a drawer, and pulled out some books. "If you want, you can read these. They're some of my favorites."

"You like to read too?" Hector asked.

"Of course," she said. "That's why I'm a teacher."

One of the books took place during the American Civil War, and Hector found himself marching with General Grant and the troops. They were hungry and tired. When they stopped to rest, Grant looked at Hector and said, "We need to advance by sundown."

"Okay," Hector said. "If you want, I can read ahead and tell you what happens."

"You're a weird kid," said Grant.

Then, Grant looked around, leaned into Hector, and said, "You know General Hooker? I don't like that guy one bit."

In another book, Albert Einstein was pacing the patent office where he was a clerk, and he was thinking about his theory of relativity, but Hector didn't understand his thoughts. They were way over his head, and he was about to put down the book when Einstein looked at him and said, "Is something wrong, young man?"

"I don't understand anything," Hector said.

The genius grabbed his coat from a hook and said, "Come on. Let's take a walk."

"Imagine yourself chasing after a beam of light," he said. "No matter how fast you go, the light will always move at the same speed away from you. You can never catch it. Isn't that odd? Even if you move at the speed of light, light will move away from you at the speed of light."

One day Miss Pickles asked the class to name some generals in the Civil War, and Hector said them all.

"Wow, that's pretty impressive, Hector."

"Grant didn't like General Hooker."

"How do you know?"

"He told me. I mean, I read it in a book."

One day Hector went back to visit Horace, who was happily eating pizza in a carrot patch. "There you are!" said Horace. "I thought you would never come back."

"You're my friend," Hector said.

"What about your other friend? You said I could meet her."

"Okay. Just let me figure it out."

He put down the book and found himself seated in his regular chair in the library. He picked up the book with Quark and read.

"Hey," she said. "What do you want to do today?"

"I want you to meet my friend Horace. He's a bunny."

"Okay," she said. "Where is he?"

Hector held both books in his hands, one in each, with the pages open. He looked at Horace and said, "Come on. Can you step into this other book?"

Horace tried to step out of the pages, but only a tip of his very long ear made it to the other side. When he tried to step out of his book, he found himself on the next page.

Hector looked at Quark and said, "Maybe you could fly out of the page."

She tried flying to the very top of the page, but she ended up on the bottom of the next page.

"There's got to be a way," Hector said.

Sometimes the best ideas come when you're not even thinking about the problem. Hector was walking to school. It was a cool morning. The sky was clear and the city seemed almost peaceful for once. He could hear the birds chirping in the trees. He could hear the laughter of children, the shifting of gears on delivery trucks. He felt happy, like he wanted that moment to last for a very long time.

That's when the idea came to him.

If anyone could understand this problem, it would be a genius. Einstein!

Hector had read that book about his life, so he picked it up and walked right into it. The young genius was at the patent office in Bern, writing equations on a napkin and thinking about the speed of light.

"Einstein? Can I ask you a question?"

The genius looked up. He focused hard to see who was talking to him, and when he recognized Hector, he smiled. "Of course, Hector. You can ask me anything."

Hector explained the problem, how he couldn't get Horace out of his world and into the world of Quark.

Einstein got his coat from a hook and led Hector onto the streets of Bern, and they walked down avenues and across squares as they talked. Hector noticed there were clocks everywhere in the buildings. It was 10:10.

"What you need is a wormhole."

"A what?"

"You need to find a passage from one world to another. If both your friends Horace and Quark are in the world of your imagination, then *you* are your own wormhole."

"I don't understand," said Hector.

"Every book is a wormhole," said the genius.

If he wanted Horace and Quark to meet, all he had to do is write a book about it.

He'd write everything, what they say to each other, what they would do, and then he would read what he wrote and enter into a story of his own creation.

When he got out of school that day, he went to the library, found a table, and started writing. He could create anything he wanted. Did he want to be a king? He could write it. Did he want a full moon? He could write it. If he wanted to fly, he could write it.

He wrote and wrote and wrote. He wrote a story about how Horace and Quark became friends. "You guys want to meet my friend Bigger?" he asked. "He's an elephant."

"Absolutely!" they said.

So he wrote Bigger into the story.

"What do you guys want to do?" asked Hector.

"Let's go hide in the trees," said Bigger, looking around to make sure no poachers could see him. He was so big next to his tiny friends, especially standing side-by-side with the bunny, who barely reached past one of Bigger's toes.

"We don't need to hide anymore," said Quark. "Hector's writing our story now."

"I know what we can do!" said Horace.

They all said, "Yes, we know. You want cheese pizza."

"Yeah, that sounds great!" said Horace.

The other three rolled their eyes.

Quark yelled, "Let's go visit other stories!" and everyone yelled agreement and they found themselves surrounded by a circle of trees in a meadow at night. Three girls in white dresses danced under the moonlight, and they all danced together and laughed.

"I want to see a castle," said Hector, and in the distance a castle appeared.

"Let's go!" they all yelled.

"Want to ride on my back?" Bigger asked the others.

They all jumped on, and they trotted along the path and screamed with delight when Bigger bucked a bit to make them bounce.

One day, when his mom and dad were out somewhere together (they "made up" as much as they fought), he was sitting at the table in the kitchen writing his story when his sister walked in carrying a stack of books.

She stood there watching Hector, like she was disappointed to see him. Then she sat across from him.

"What's up?" Hector asked.

"Nothing," she said. "I need a place to study. This is where I usually come when Mom and Dad are out."

She opened a thick math book and bent over it. "I hate math," said Hector.

"Well, math is pretty cool, I guess. I mean, no matter what, there's a right answer and there's a wrong answer. You don't have to guess what's right, you just have to figure it out. I wish life were like that. You know what I mean?"

"I think so," said Hector.

Just then the doorbell rang, and they looked at each other. "Who could it be?" asked his sister, concerned. No one ever knocked on their door but the police or angry neighbors.

Hector went to the door, looked in the peephole, and saw a distorted version of his friends Horace, Quark, and Bigger. He opened the door and was excited to see them on the other side. Beyond them was not the city, but miles and miles of rolling blue mountains. Hector's sister stood next to her brother, looking at his friends.

"What the heck is going on?" she said.

"Hey, guys," said Hector. "This is my sister."

"Let's go play," said Quark.

"Come on out!" said Horace.

"Bring your sister," said Bigger.

"Hector who are these . . . uh . . . ?"

"Come out!" they said. "Come out!"

Hector looked at his sister, whose face went soft, like she suddenly understood something beautiful. She looked at Hector.

"Let's go," he said, and they stepped out the door.

# YOGA

After my wife died, I tried yoga, in Santa Monica.

I was the only man in a class of limber, in-shape women. They all had their own mats, but I had to borrow one from the house.

Minutes into it, I'm soaking in sweat.

I couldn't do stretches. I couldn't touch my toes, no downward dog.

The yoga instructor, an Asian woman in her twenties, asked me if I was all right, like I was going to die. She was worried about me.

"Do you want to rest awhile?" she asked.

The class was silent, looking at me. I was covered in sweat, my clothes dripping. "I need this," I said, stretching so it hurt.

# PART FOUR

# ALLIGATOR PLAZA

*"One minute I want to remember. The next minute I want to live*
*in the land of forgetting."*

B. A. SÁENZ

To paraphrase our city's most famous writer, everything begins and ends at The Tap. It's a downtown bar, right across the street from a giant sculpture of an Aztec calendar, and for three, sometimes four, sometimes more nights a week I was there, marking off the days of my life.

This story begins there, on a regular night. Maybe it was a Tuesday.

La Bestia was working, and she never asked if I wanted another Lone Star, she just knew when I did, and she'd put a full one in front of me. But not tonight.

She leaned over the bar to whisper something to me. She was huge, like Shrek, and she had these big earrings made of silver that hung and swung from her ears, thick pickaxes, the kind that miners use to break into rock looking for gold. That was La Bestia in a nut-shell, always looking for gold.

This night, she said to me, "Want to make some money?"

She knew I needed it. I was a second-grade schoolteacher with alimony and child support, and I ran out of money after the first two weeks of the month, and that night it was, as I recall, about the twenty-second of that month.

"What do I got to do?"

"See those Bliss boys?" she asked, and I looked across the bar at the two soldiers, their close-cut hair and red necks. They were sitting at the bar drinking beers and doing shots of tequila. Standing between them was Mike the one-armed African American cowboy. He was in The Tap almost as much as I was. He was whispering into the ears of the Bliss boys, and they seemed amused, occasionally laughing at what he said. Mike made people laugh all the time, and they bought him beers.

"Do you see them boys?"

"Yeah," I said. "How come you didn't notice I need another beer?"

"Just listen!" she said. "If you do what I ask, you'll have a glass of beer that'll never go empty."

Las Bestia was like that, loved talking in metaphors. When she was a little girl, she wanted to be a nun.

"You mean I could drink a bottle, put it down, and when I pick it up again it'll be full and cold and ready to chug-a-lug?"

"Bravo," she said, sarcastically. "You're a genius. Now here's what I want you to do." She leaned in, and I could have sworn both the Bliss boys looked at us, as if they knew what we were talking about.

La Bestia told me that those boys were here to pick up something, and she wanted me to take them there so they could get it. All I had to do was walk them down the street to the corner Wells Fargo ATM and type in the digits 5277.

"Five-two-seven-seven," I said.

"Don't forget that, 5277. You should write it down."

"I got a photographic memory. I never forget."

"Well, you put in 5277."

"Five-two-seven-seven," I repeated. "Then what happens?"

"Then a man in a white van is going to pull up on the curb. When you see that, you get out of there fast, and then you come back here and get your money."

"That's it?"

"That's it."

"How much money?"

"Ten grand."

"You're lying."

She leaned in real close and growled at me, showing me her teeth. Her breath smelled good, like lavender or sandalwood. "I don't mess around," she said.

When she stood up straight, I don't know how she did it, but there was full bottle of Lone Star in front of me, and the empty bottle was gone.

I chugged it quick, felt the rush of the beer in my bloodstream, and then I put the empty down on the bar with a *tap tap tap.*

Before I could leave, La Bestia made a sound for me to stop: *Psst!*

"Let me give you this," she said. It was a compass, Army issue, and it was open and the little needle was pointing north.

"Why do I need this?"

But she was gone, taking orders from a cocktail waitress, a little blonde lady who was so short she had to reach up to put empty glasses on the bar.

I went outside and crossed the street and waited under the darkness of the Aztec calendar. Desert nights can be hot, and this one was the worst. I was starting to sweat. I wanted to smoke, but I don't smoke, so I didn't.

Not two minutes later the Bliss boys came out. They looked around, spotted me, and started to cross the street. I walked the other way, across a narrow alley and onto the sidewalk. I could feel them behind me. I passed a wall that had a metal door, and written on it was PROHIBIDO EL PASO.

When I got to the ATM, I was about to punch in the code, but then I couldn't remember what it was.

I tried my best and punched in 5598 and 5589 and 5599, 5600, 5601, but I couldn't get it. The Bliss boys were crossing the street toward me, and I put in anything that came to mind, 5544, 5537, 5390, 9087, 2666, but nothing happened. Then the soldiers were standing there right next to me, towering over me. I'm just a short Mexican man.

I put in 4467, 3289, 6343, 9893, but nothing happened.

"There is problem?" one of the Bliss boys asked, and I was surprised that he had what sounded like a German accent.

"Do you not have the code?" he asked me threateningly.

"Of course I have the code! You guys wait right here. I'm going to get it."

"Why don't you have it with you?" screamed one of the Bliss boys, like a Nazi movie cliché.

"I brought the wrong one," I said. "I accidentally brought last week's code. The codes change every week. They're very careful about . . ."

"This is not good!" said one of the boys.

"Wait right here! Look, if you guys want, while I'm getting the code you can walk one block in that direction and you'll see the plaza.

It's really nice. There's alligators! And you can feed them. I'll be right back."

The Bliss boys looked at each other. "They let you feed the alligators?" one said to the other.

I went back down the street, crossed the avenue, and went into the blinking neon of The Tap.

I went back to my stool, and I saw it, right where it should be, a cold, brand-new bottle of Lone Star.

La Bestia at the other end of the bar was handing Mike the one-armed cowboy a bottle of Bud. She looked over at me and winked.

# IT'S THE ESCHATOLOGY!

The young man parked his car in the parking lot of ¡El Super!, the gigantic Mexican grocery store that was the anchor for the Viva Villa Plaza Shopping Center, a strip mall on the corner of two busy avenues in El Paso, Texas. He walked across the parking lot to the little storefront recruiting office, thinking he could be in boot camp by the end of the week, but when he walked in and the electric bell chimed, the sergeant looked up from his desk and eyed the boy suspiciously, like he was a spy or a traitor.

I'd like to join the Army, said the boy. Right now. Today.

How old are you? asked the sergeant, standing up, hands on his hips. He was Arabic, and his nametag said *Sgt. Said.*

Seventeen, he answered.

The sergeant walked to the counter to face the boy, but he had to look up at him. What's your name? he asked.

José Limón, sir!

Well, Joe Lemon . . . said Said.

It's Limón.

What?

It's not Lemon, sir. Limón.

You need your parents' consent. Do you have their consent?

My mom or my dad?

Both.

But I thought . . .

The sergeant leaned into the boy and at the same time looked up at him, because he was a tall kid. Why don't you just wait until you're eighteen? That can't be too far away. You're a big boy.

The sergeant was short and had a bulge in his stomach. The boy was tall and thin with oil-black hair combed back. He smelled freshly showered.

Why do you want to join the U.S. Army, son?

To defend my country from terrorists, sir.

What terrorists?

All los pinche terrorists that threaten our great nation!

I know what you mean, son, and you know what? Joining the U.S. Army *is* the right thing to do. But let me ask you this. What if we send you to the Middle East to fight? What would you think about being in the Army then?

The boy straightened himself like he was being asked an official question by a top general. Then he belted out, I'd kick ass, sir!

You think so?

Sir, yes, sir!

I'm a sergeant, son. A sergeant. Address me as such.

Yes, sir, Sergeant Said!

The recruiting officer looked hard at the boy. Are you sure you want this?

Yes, sir!

It's not like in the movies.

No, sir!

The recruiter seemed to be thinking about something, looking absently out the storefront window, and he shrugged. Actually, I guess it is. Some of those war movies *do* portray it pretty good, like *The Hurt Locker*. Did you see that?

No, sir.

Then the sergeant seemed to step out of his military shell, and he walked back to his desk and plopped onto the seat. He twirled around as if that would help him think, and when the chair stopped, he was facing the wooden giraffe on his desk. It was painted yellow and black and had a long, slick neck. He had bought it in Africa for his wife, but she didn't like it. ¿Me traiste un jirafa? she asked, like she was offended.

But it's cute, he had said.

Cute? ¿Qué cute? she said. How about some earrings once in a while!

Now he picked up the wooden giraffe and shook it around like an ax, as if thinking about something, and then he stood up and walked to the counter. He placed the giraffe there and looked out the window, onto the vast parking lot and the desert mountains beyond. He could see the border wall, and beyond that he could see the giant sculpture the city of Juarez had commissioned from the artist Sebastian, a large red X you could see from the air, as large as the St. Louis Arch. He sighed.

Seriously. Why not wait until you're eighteen? I mean, it must be, what, two months away at the most?

Eleven months away, sir.

You *just* turned seventeen?? You're *that* young?

José stood erect, as if to show off how young he was.

Why *now*? Don't you got a girlfriend?

Er . . . not exactly.

Well that's too bad. A good wife is a good thing. Well, not a "thing," but you know what I mean. Don't you like girls?

I'd prefer not to answer that question, sir.

Really? Oh . . . okay. Well, then, answer this: Are you a U.S. citizen?

One hundred percent, sir!

Is your family from Juárez?

My grandparents are from Delicias, Chihuahua.

Ah, Delicias!

I've never been there, said the boy.

Why join now?

I want to serve my country, sir.

But why now?

The boy thought of Miss Villaseñor in front of the chalkboard writing down the day's vocabulary word, ESCHATOLOGY. He didn't remember what it meant, but he had liked the way it sounded.

Well, why now? the sergeant asked again, with a finality in his voice that said the boy better answer.

It's the eschatology, sir!

The wha?

The eschatology. I want to be part of it.

The recruiter paused. He would look up the word after the boy left.

Oh, well, that's a good answer, son. He looked the boy up and down as if trying to find a reason for José *not* to join the army. What about high school? he asked.

I can graduate early, sir! I looked into it.

Really? And you never considered college?

When I return from duty, sir! On the GI Bill, sir.

What if you don't return?

Then I'll have died honorably and proudly for the United States of America!

Resigned, as if all his arguments had failed, the sergeant went to his desk and pulled off some paperwork and handed it to José. You're not an idiot, are you?

Uh, no, sir. I mean . . . Do you mean, am I stupid?

No, like an idiot. You know, like the village idiot? Someone who has no sense. He pointed at his own head. Someone who doesn't think right in the brain, know what I'm saying?

I'm a straight A student. I'm in the marching band.

What do you play?

The tuba.

The wha?? Who plays the tuba?

It's not what I play at night, he said. My partner and I are in a punk band. It's a mixture of Norteña and classic punk. We're called The Red Aztecs. But in Spanish.

Los Aztecas Rojos, said the sergeant.

I play guitar, but I joined the marching band late, and it was the only instrument left. And since the band director needed someone big enough to hold it up, he asked me to do it.

Forget I asked, he said. Here. Have both parents sign it. If they consent, we can have you in the Army within a month.

Thank you, Sergeant Said. But he didn't leave. He stood there. Sir, can I ask you a question?

Sure, but quit calling me, sir. It's *Sergeant.*

Sergeant Said, can I ask you . . .

*Sah-eed.* It's not pronounced *Said.* It's pronounced *Sah-eed.*

Well, Sergeant Sah-eed. You seem reluctant to have me join, Sergeant Sah-eed. Can I ask why?

Said walked right up to the boy, his nose inches from the boy's nose, only he had to look up into the boy's nostrils. I want you to know what you're facing. I want you to know . . . He looked out the window at the X. Someone had told him, maybe his wife, that it symbolized all the deaths in Ciudad Juárez, from the disappeared women to the drug wars that killed thousands.

So much death. Judgment. Afterlife. He sighed. There's a lot of bad hombres out there, he said.

I can fight, said the boy.

You're asking to join the greatest army the world has ever known, to protect the greatest country the world has ever known. This ain't no video game. He whispered an aside. By the way, the *ain't* was intentional.

Got it, sir . . . Sergeant!

We need men who know what they face! Not little muchachos wanting to get their college paid for. There will be death. There will be death. There will be death. If not you, the guy next to you. ¿Me entiendes?

Yes, Sergeant Sah-eed!

That was when they heard the explosion. Said instinctively ducked down on the floor for cover, but the boy just stood there, looking at the shattered window.

Fascist pigs! they heard.

Someone had thrown a large rock into the window, and he was running away, through the parking lot, past the ¡Super! It looked like a blond kid, a teenager. He was laughing like a crazy person.

By the time Said got up off the floor, José was gone. He looked up and saw the boy chasing after the vandal, running though the cars so swiftly and gracefully that he looked like a giraffe—sprinting across the Serengeti.

# SIX COWS IN A SPACESHIP

The young chair told everyone his idea: They needed to get out of that building.

It was crumbling, uninsulated, and cold, and the room was lit by a bulb on the ceiling swinging from a wire that shifted shadows like a trite detail from a novel.

"This place is a dump," he said, his shadow sliding back and forth on the wall behind him. "There's hungry mice everywhere, eating coffee cake crumbs we leave behind. I say we find someplace else to meet."

There was much discussion.

The middle-aged woman in the green pantsuit with a blonde page-boy haircut made an amendment:

The next place had to be green, she said, socially responsible, and all the products they used—coffee, snacks—should be sustainable and from independent producers. "And for god's sake," she said. "Let's quit using Styrofoam!"

There was much debate.

In the end, everyone agreed to the proposal and the amendment, except for the foreign guy. He didn't understand English but thought he did, and he couldn't believe what he had heard.

He stood up, angry and indignant.

"I can't believe what you are saying!" he said in his thick foreign accent.

"Asking us to cut off our fingers and feed them to hungry mice is a stupid idea. And worse yet," he said, pointing to the woman in the green pantsuit. "Your idea of taking the mice and skinning them with a green knife and taking out their eyes—Really disgusting!"

There was much confusion.

"Uh, we're not sure what you're talking about," said the chair, speaking for everyone. He was tall and bald and had a red beard and wore skinny jeans. "We all just want to get along here, right?"

"You may think so! But no! I will not put on high heels just to please you!" said the foreign man.

The woman in the green pantsuit said, "Maybe he doesn't understand English that well."

"Oh, no!" said the foreigner. "I will not drink from your cistern!"

"Okay," she said. "My mistake."

"Anyway, we'll talk about this later," said the young chair. "Let's get through this agenda."

He put his head down to read the next item, and his shiny scalp reflected the room and the doors and windows like an Escher drawing.

He stroked his long, red beard.

"The funds in our reserve account look pretty good, so I'd like to use some to pay Zapata, the caterer who worked our teach-in last summer. He keeps sending us nasty reminders that we haven't paid."

A man in a wheelchair wearing sunglasses and a U.S. Army jacket added his opinion: "I say let them complain. If we keep the reserve account going for a few more years, maybe we can get into that new building on the river."

"What??" said the foreign guy, so incredulous he was practically spitting. "You want to take forty puppies—little baby dowgies?—and dump them into the river??"

There was much confusion.

People looked at each other for answers. The woman in the green pantsuit asked, "Excuse me?"

The chair, twirling a finger through his red beard, said, "Maybe we're not seeing each other's points here, because . . ."

"Objection!!" yelled the foreign guy. "I am NOT zombie Nazi!"

An old black man sitting next to a young Latina with short hair said to her, "Did he really call him a zombie Nazi?"

She shrugged her shoulders. "Probably," she said.

"That's a shame," he said, shaking his head.

"I'm tired of how these people treat us," said the Latina.

"Like we're invisible," said the old black man, nodding his head.

"Look," said the chair. "I say we postpone this meeting until next week."

A svelte old man standing in the back wearing an expensive Nike sweat suit and wireless Bose earphones said, "Can we meet at Starbucks next time? Then maybe we can have good coffee for once."

He held up a sad Styrofoam cup.

"Who wants to meet at Starbucks?" asked the chair.

"No! No! No!" yelled the foreign man. "I will NOT gather six cows, put them into spaceships, fly them into the stars, and blow them up!"

The woman in the green pantsuit said, "Okay, I'm done with this crap. I'm leaving."

"You're going to put crack in baby food!?" yelled the foreign guy. "Why?? Can you imagine those little babies crawling around all wired? Think of the mothers!!!"

"Yeah!" said the Latina. "Think of the mothers!"

"Crack is killing our people!" said the black man.

The old man in the sweat suit and earphones said, "Enough of this stupidity! This immigrant obviously doesn't speak English. He has no place here."

There was a communal "Ah!"

No one could believe what the old man had said, but secretly, most of them understood why he said it. He was frustrated, they thought. He didn't really mean it.

"Now, Jon," said the woman in the green pantsuit, "that's inappropriate and you know it."

There was much talking and yelling.

The black man and the Latina watched it all.

"Go back to your country!" screamed the old man in the sweat suit, crushing the Styrofoam cup in his fist and tossing the pieces.

"Here it goes," said the Latina, shaking her head. The foreigner slowly walked to the old man. There was much tension.

The foreigner stopped in front of the tall old man and said, right to his face:

"Finally! A reasonable person. Thank you! I, too, think you are a man of honor, and I appreciate what you're saying about my looks." He winked at him. "And yes, I iron them myself."

# THE TRUTH ABOUT THE WALL®

*The great wall alone would for the first time in the age of human beings create a secure foundation for a new Tower of Babel.*

KAFKA

The Wall* isn't a futuristic metallic wall like they show in their advertising, shiny metal reaching Babel-like to the clouds and curving around the globe. In fact, it's not a wall at all, but it was named years ago when three entrepreneurs started a firewall company that protected your personal computer from malware, but now that most users store their data in the cloud, the company expanded to become the number-one data storage business in the world.

Now, The Wall* expands across 17,000 acres in rural Iowa, a rectangular warehouse the size of a town. Inside the structure, you see row after row of huge black boxes with flashing blue and red and green lights. They reach as far as the eye can see, and each box contains billions and billions of bytes of information from customers, corporate and personal and government, as well as former costumers who cancelled their service and those who signed up for the free trial but never subscribed.

There's space enough to store billions and billions of yottabytes of information, more than all the information since the dawn of humankind (which could frankly be stored in a few of those black boxes). In each unit there are perhaps eighty billion terabytes of photos alone, millions of weddings, parties, trips to the park, children wandering off in parks, naked husbands and wives, cats curling up on beds or looking cutely out of empty suitcases, dogs looking up and begging for bacon, selfies taken in front of the Golden Gate Bridge, the Hollywood sign, the Eiffel Tower, the zócalo in Mexico City, Joe's Crab Shack in Maple Grove, Minnesota, the Great Wall of China, the London Eye, so many images stored inside those boxes that if you were to put them all together like a puzzle you would see every corner of the earth, sometimes a single spot from multiple angles and different lighting, morning light, night light, afternoon light, overcast light barely breaking through the clouds, light that shines on a rice farm in Thailand, on a stage in a theater, and millions and millions of smiling faces, frowning faces, surprised faces, selfie faces with duck lips, faces in front of world monuments trying to look happy so they can post on social media and show their friends that they saw the Mona Lisa or the statue of David, Lenin's tomb, Carlsbad Caverns, Mount Rushmore, Disneyland, the beautiful blue Danube, St. Paul's Cathedral, Auschwitz.

There are photos of cars, bikes, cups of coffee, fences, masks, guns, cash, flowerpots with no flowers, flowerpots with flowers, flowerpots with weeds, flowerpots with dead flowers, flowerpots with puppies sticking their heads out, sunflowers, cactus, bushes, trees, cattails, new tires, old tires, pots and pans, paycheck stubs, and all kinds of food, tacos, lobsters, double cheeseburgers with avocado sticking out the side, New York deli sandwiches with meat piled high, vegetarian sandwiches, plates of hummus, olives, cherries in a white bowl.

When the average person takes an image of their food at a restaurant so they can post it on Facebook or Instagram they shoot the plate six to ten times, often more than that, and although only one of the images might end up being shared, the person does not delete the others, and why should they? With The Wall' they have enough storage space for a billion meals.

A terabyte alone could store every photograph ever taken by Cartier-Bresson, Arbus, Irturbide, Mary Allen Mark, and the rest of the world's famous photographers.

So why not take multiple shots of fruit in bowls, pies in windows, and windows?

Windows of office buildings and tenement buildings, windows looking onto gardens, onto rivers, onto mountains; windows framing the full moon, windows looking out on snow-covered backyards. So many windows in so many houses and buildings and cars and so many cars and trucks and buses and motorcycles and bicycles and skateboards and hover machines and running shoes and feet.

Any object you can think of has been photographed and stored in The Wall', a compass, a brush, a defibrillator in the airport, and things you wouldn't think of, calliopes, Bergonic chairs, electroretinograms, zultanites, so many images that if unlimited computing power existed to put them all together side-by-side, you would see the face of God.

The Wall° doesn't only store photos but billions of videos, billions of audio files, from the Beatles' first album to the audio file of children singing patriotic songs for their school play, dedicated to their love of country. Everything spoken into a voice memo app is backed up in the cloud, comedians practicing jokes, poets reading their works aloud, rants and diatribes—in any language you can think of.

And there are billions of documents people put there for safe-keeping, letters to airlines complaining about late flights, love letters, breakup letters, freshman compositions, and enough poems to fill one trillion and two volumes of poetry, fictional stories, entries from personal journals, words words words no one has ever read and some that millions have read, the first drafts of works of literature, like *Aristotle and Dante Discover the Secrets of the Universe, Your Daughters Are Looking at the Moon*, the first draft of *Todo eso es yo*, and there are second drafts and paragraphs, passages and sentences of fiction that will never be used, half-drawn-out characters, and millions of plays and sitcoms and teleplays, and there are feature film screenplays, thousands and thousands of them so heartbreakingly beautiful but that will never be made into films.

And lists.

Before people go to the store to buy things, they write what they need on their notes app, and they rarely bother to delete them from the cloud, and even if they do delete them, The Wall' will hold them forever. There are lists from mothers giving daughters and sons chores they need to do, "mow the lawn, clean the refrigerator, wear bras, quit wearing your sister's bra," lists they don't even need to think about deleting, because the average person cannot in a lifetime take up one terabyte of storage space, the minimum storage you can get as an individual subscriber.

Of the average 5K gigabytes most ordinary people use in a lifetime, 4K of it is stuff they don't even know is in the cloud, things they will never read again, like a love letter from a man named Pierre Duchamp to an African woman he saw thirty years ago in a shop window in

Marseilles, a city he was visiting only for the day. She worked the counter at a clothing store for babies, and he could never forget her. Before he left the city, he tried to find the shop so he could see her one last time, but he walked all over the city, through streets and alleys and across plazas, but he couldn't find the shop, as if the city were a trickster labyrinth hiding its most valued treasure. Throughout the years he imagined her name was Sylvia, so that's what he called her when he imagined her. Sylvia, he would say to himself, but he never saw her again.

One morning, three days before he would retire from his job at the prison, he gets so anguished that he never spoke to Sylvia that for the first time he writes to her, an email, and he imagines that she will read it. Of course, no one will ever will read it, but the draft is stored in The Wall˚ with other personal letters no one will ever read.

Including this unsent email written in Spanish by a mother to her daughter.

*Sara,*

*I don't know if you will ever read this, but I am going to try hard to send it to you, since I know I will probably never see you again. They stopped us at the border. They stopped us, and they took you away. They put you with other children, and as much as I tried, they wouldn't give me any information about you. I'm so sorry. All I wanted was a better life for you. I hope that you are somewhere better, that somehow you got out and moved on to a better life. I'm so sorry. I'm sorry. I'm sorry. You are precious. You are the world to me.*

*I don't know how long I have left, but I will spend the rest of my life looking for you. I promise.*

*I'm sorry.*

       *Love Mom (please!)*

# ACKNOWLEDGMENTS

I'd like to thank Jolène Monet Espinoza, my life partner, for encouraging me to write these stories and constantly supporting this book, even at those times when I didn't believe in it. Thank you for letting me read these stories aloud to you.

And thanks to Eliyah Lara for putting up with my weird ideas and imagination. I love sharing stories with you.

I'd like to also thank Maceo Montoya, Kenneth R. Chacón, Carlos Espinoza, and Paula Cucurella.

Thank-you to Mindy, my copy editor. I don't know how you do it!

And of course, I'd like to thank my two cats, Bacon and Sofía, who were often there next to me as I tapped on the keys of my laptop writing these stories. They would tilt their heads and look at me, encourage me with purrs and meows, and sometimes they sat on the keyboard preventing me from working. They kept me rooted in the moment.

# ABOUT THE AUTHOR

DANIEL CHACÓN is a professor of creative writing at the University of Texas, El Paso. He earned an MFA in creative writing from the University of Oregon. He is the author of the novel *The Cholo Tree*, as well as three previous collections of short stories, including *Hotel Juárez: Stories, Rooms and Loops*, which won both the 2014 PEN Oakland Award for Literary Excellence and the Tejas NACCS Award for Best Book of Fiction for 2013; and *Unending Rooms*, which won the 2008 Hudson Prize. He was a co-editor of *The Last Supper of Chicano Heroes*, and his writing has been featured in numerous anthologies of Latinx literature, including *Lengua Fresca: Latinos Writing on the Edge* and *Latino Boom: An Anthology of U.S. Latino Literature*.